www.HarperLin.com

Pawsitively Dead

A Wonder Cats Mystery
Book 2

by Harper Lin

This is a work of fiction. Names, characters, organizations,places, events, and incidents are either products of the author's imagination or are used fictitiously.

PAWSITIVELY DEAD Copyright © 2015 by Harper Lin.
All rights reserved.

ISBN-13: 978-1987859218
ISBN-10: 1987859219

Contents

1. The Anniversary

Death was a part of life. You didn't need to be a witch to know that. Witches might sometimes deal with it differently than non-witches, though it didn't seem so on the anniversary of my parents' death.

Before I left to visit them in the graveyard, my aunt Astrid and cousin Bea were varnishing the mezzanine in the newly rebuilt Brew-Ha-Ha, our family cafe.

Aunt Astrid was spry and clear-eyed at sixty-seven, always ready to roll up her sleeves and renovate. To people who didn't know her well, she was usually just an older woman with wispy swathes of blond-gray hair and loose tie-dyed dresses who always seemed to have a distant look in her eyes. Usually it was because she was remembering the future. Non-witches underestimated her; she was actually a lot sharper than she looked.

My cousin Bea approached the varnishing of the mezzanine more studiously, drawing from everything she'd ever read about primers and painting and architecture. She was the bookish sort and remembered everything she read. She was also beautiful, big-hearted, popular, and two years younger than me. I couldn't be jealous of her even if I tried. She wore her heart on her sleeve, and she healed everybody she touched. And I meant that literally. Healing was Bea's witch talent.

The Brew-Ha-Ha had been the most popular cafe in our hometown of Wonder Falls before the cafe had practically burned to a crisp. I was hanging a photo of our late baker on the wall behind the bar. Poor Ted. He had been tragically caught in the fires and passed away. He never knew his employers were three witches.

"Cath!" a familiar voice called my name.

That would be the elated voice of my childhood friend Min. He didn't know I was a witch either. Not many people did. Min and I had lost contact after he went out of town for college, and now that he was back, I was getting to know him again.

That day, he wore a brand-new T-shirt and jeans, looking a lot nicer than he used to in our childhood days. Probably because he'd sold his business and become obscenely wealthy. He was never a braggart about it though. He was even nice enough to come over and help take over my role in the renovation of the Brew-Ha-Ha while I had to step away for the morning.

"You look ready to work up a sweat," I said when he came through the door. He gave me a light hug in greeting. "Thanks for coming in to help."

He peered through the bars of the mezzanine and waved hello at Bea and Aunt Astrid.

"Hey, Min!" Bea called.

Aunt Astrid added, "Just open the windows while you're down there, would you? Getting some air in here would help this all dry faster."

"Right." He made for the nearest window, stopped himself, and grinned at me, almost shyly. "Your hair's different. Nice, I mean. Not that it was bad the old way."

I'd had my dark ringlets straightened for the occasion—for two occasions, technically. "Samantha really wanted me to get it dyed or styled like, well, in her style."

"You went to Perry's Parlor just for a hair straightening?" Min laughed with incredulity.

Samantha Perry, a friend of one of Aunt Astrid's friends, had opened a hair salon in town. Samantha was almost fifty, but she was a real live wire and a rebel. I laughed with him. "I'm all for supporting small businesses in my hometown! My head just can't support a spiked green mohawk."

"That's what I want to do now. Support small businesses here." He quickly added, "I mean, not just because you mentioned it and I'm trying to copy your opinion or one-up you or anything like that."

I stopped myself from raising an eyebrow at his backpedaling. The Greenstones and the Parks had always been like family. Even if we hadn't seen each other in years, what was Min so nervous about?

He continued rambling. "I mean that supporting the locals is what I want to do, but I don't know. Putting my life to use is just something I've been thinking about since Tommy passed."

Thomas Thompson had graduated from Wonder Falls High the same year as Min and me. We didn't even know him well enough to call him Tommy, really, but he had become the pride of the town when the news network he worked for won a Michener Award. Then it turned out he won the award for an expose on the torture of prisoners of war under the Canadian Forces, and he became an embarrassment instead. That was, until he was caught in crossfire in some faraway war-torn desert and shot to death. From then on, he had been a hero.

"War correspondent is a dangerous job," I remarked.

Min nodded. "I don't mean I want to end up like Tommy. I just want to make a difference in our community, you know?"

I sighed. Our community. "I doubt anyone in this town would take too kindly to an investor, actually. They might view it as condescending. People here have a lot of pride."

I didn't really know why Min had even come back to Wonder Falls. If I hadn't been there to protect him, school life would have been unbearable, and even looking back at that time, we couldn't really call it happy. Min's father had impossibly high standards that Min could never quite meet, and Min's mother tended to be overbearing. He must have found a balance between the two though, and maybe he stayed in town just to be around his family. Family was the reason why I'd never left.

"I'm sure you'll think of something," I said then followed up with a reminder about the windows. "You know, it would be nice to have your problem, having the option of not working and doing whatever you want."

I put on my jacket, draped a black picnic blanket over one arm, and called my farewells to Bea and Aunt Astrid on my way out.

Death was a part of life, and life went on. When a mezzanine needed varnishing, we rolled up our sleeves and opened the windows to let out the fumes. We laughed about hairstyles and planned for a future where we could make our mark on the world and make it a better place to live. That day didn't have to be so full of doom just because it was my parents' death anniversary. But unfortunately, it was.

2. Graveyard Surprises

I walked down to the corner of Ebb and Eddy and considered that my shoes were formal but sensible enough to visit my parents' tombs. The sunshine shone pale yellow though the early morning air. I thought that I might as well take the path through the meadow to the graveyard.

That turned out to be a terrible idea. I wore all black and was sweltering by the time I was halfway down the path.

Wonder Falls didn't have a proper park. On one side of the path, children ran about, shouting in delight, playing hide-and-seek and other games, as their parents and guardians watched from picnic blankets or short boulders that served as seats. On the other side of the path, a Dalmatian strained against its leash as it snarled and barked at me. Gillian Hyllis, the local fire chief and the dog's owner, waved at me apologetically.

With my witch talent of communicating with animals, I joined my mind to the Dalmatian's and commanded it to quiet down. I sensed puzzlement in return, which translated in human to, "You smell like cat!"

Of course I did. My cat, Treacle, had helped me pick my outfit. That had been after taking him to the grooming salon, so at least my clothes didn't smell of alleyway or garbage or whatever cats got into when they insisted upon straying. Treacle was a black cat, so if any fallen hairs had stuck to my clothes, most humans wouldn't notice.

A lot of animals had senses keener than human senses, but if that dog—like a lot of dogs—couldn't be polite, then I ought to have just stuck to communicating with cats, as I usually did.

The unpaved meadow path sloped downhill and led into an abandoned orchard. The sprawling branches cast mottled shadows over the slope. A river stirred up a cool breeze as the water rushed to the distant falls somewhere over the horizon.

Our town was named for the falls, and my family had a bond with the Maid of the Mist that reached back for generations. How could I explain the Maid of the Mist? Some people were between worlds, and she was one of them.

The Greenstones were familiar with her, so we called her, as well as other people we could not explain to humans, our Familiar. The Maid of the Mist could take all manner of different forms, but something about being a witch meant that we recognized her every time. However, she didn't show up to me anymore, although she used to when I was a young girl, playing in forests and nature settings like where I was now.

I stayed a little longer in the orchard, looking for the right sort of wildflowers in the shade. I found them and walked on toward the graveyard, and on the other side of the stone bridge, I saw the St. Bernard dog by the river bank. It sank its giant paws into the shallows and lapped up the water. Part of a leash hung from its collar. It must have done what the Dalmatian had been doing, straining against the leash, but its leash must've been too weak or the dog too strong.

"Hey, there," I said. "Someone must be missing you. Come over here."

The dog looked up, startled, then backed away and whimpered. I hesitated going after the St. Bernard. I didn't want to mud wrestle with a dog the size of an adolescent bear all the way to the animal shelter. Instead, I used my powers, but when I tried to connect our minds, the dog did the magic-force equivalent of pushing me away. Then the dog bolted. Some animals were afraid of magic powers.

I took my phone out of my jacket pocket and called the Wonder Falls animal shelter. Old Murray, who ran the animal shelter, was out that day. His teenaged grandson, Cody, answered for him, so I told Cody about the St. Bernard on the loose.

Then I continued my walk to the graveyard from the meadow. The entrance was a waist-high, whitewashed wooden swinging door between two poles. The place was hidden, but everybody in town just knew where it was.

When I got to my parents' shared grave, a black cat with a star-shaped scar on his forehead sat before the tombstone, as if he were reading the names. Stella Greenstone. Gordon Greenstone.

The black cat's name was Treacle. My cat.

"Everyone's out walking their dog," I warned Treacle as I unfolded the picnic blanket. Treacle yawned and stretched over to sit with me.

None of the dogs in town had ever bothered him, but I knew he would appreciate the warning. Treacle was a street cat. He was clever. He could dodge dogs of any size, but then again, cats were smarter than dogs.

"Hi, Mom and Dad. I'm sorry I'm late," I said to the grave. "Mallows are hard to find when the meadow's crowded. It was nice to be out with everyone though."

I talked to my parents in my head after that. I didn't want anybody passing by to overhear the real story behind Ted's death or how we were rebuilding the cafe as fast as we could. But not too fast—we had to restrict our magic because we didn't want any townspeople wondering how we were getting it done in such a short amount of time. I also caught my parents up on other news, such as Thomas Thompson's recent death.

I wondered if witchcraft was really enough. We could protect people who weren't witches from evil beings and evil magic from other dimensions—other dimensions that only witches knew the ways of. But what could we do about the evil in this dimension, like wars? Unlike Ted, Thomas's death hadn't involved magic at all.

I sighed to my parents and stopped my train of thoughts, hoping I wasn't being too much of a downer. Treacle comforted me by putting his front paws on my knee. I stroked his head.

"I was orphaned," I said out loud. "Aunt Astrid was widowed. How do we protect ourselves from the pain of death?"

In any case, I blamed myself a little for my parents' deaths. They had, after all, been fighting the monster under my bed. A literal monster.

Aunt Astrid always tried to hammer into me that my mother was only doing her duty as a witch, protecting everybody in town from the evil thing masquerading as a child's imaginary monster. I didn't know enough to believe her though. Not until I found myself taking on the same duties. As witches, we had to do our best, but sometimes tragedies happened as a result of our jobs. I just had to do better, in whatever situation came my way, and hope for the best.

I thought, as I laid the mallow flowers on the grave, that I would be ready to do what needed to be done. That was what being a witch meant.

Then I noticed where the sun was in the sky, how bright its light was over the graveyard. The morning was going much faster than usual. I also realized that I'd forgotten to bring a packed lunch like I usually did on the anniversary.

I left Treacle on the blanket, conveying "I'll be right back" with my mind. I would swing by the delicatessen and grab something. I stood and fumbled through my jacket pockets, hoping I'd brought some cash, when something unusually magenta caught my eye beside the statue of an angel I was facing. The magenta was too glossy to be a bunch of wildflowers. It was human hair.

All of a sudden, even the sunshine felt cold.

"Excuse me," I called out, approaching the statue slowly. When I looked around the statue, I saw the body—the dress, the shoes. "Are you okay?" *Please be drunk. Please be sleeping, whoever you—*

The magenta hair turned into lime green where it fell on the ground and neon orange where it fell over her face. The neon orange hair over her nose and mouth wasn't moving with her breath. I stood still, holding my own breath, hoping I was mistaken, hoping she would breathe and blink and wake up.

"Samantha?"

I bent down to take a closer look at her face. Even though no one else in town would have that hair, I had to make sure. Unfortunately, it was Samantha.

I stepped back, slowly at first, then I stumbled a good distance away. I plunged my hand into the other pocket of my jacket and fumbled until I found my cell phone. Even with my hands beginning to shake, I turned my phone on and dialed the Wonder Falls police station.

"Wonder Falls Police," said a familiar voice on the other line.

"Blake!" I cried. "I'm at the graveyard. I saw Samantha lying here—Samantha Perry. I—I think she's dead!"

Blake maintained his professional cool. "We'll be right on over. Just calm down, and don't move anything."

I took a breath and choked on something that I smelled.

"Cath?" said Blake. "Are you all right?"

I answered with a cough. "Something reeks!"

I turned around, and I saw what must have caused the stench. It was a pile of bones, a skeleton essentially, with gray, brittle skin stretched over it. The lips had decayed enough that the skull seemed to grin at me. "Uh-oh."

"What is it?"

I said, "You might want to bring backup."

3. An Empty Casket

B lake and Jake arrived on the scene, and they had listened, bringing backup with them, along with the medical examiner. I met Detectives Blake Samberg, Jake Williams, and Marlene Strauss, the medical examiner, at the entrance and told them why I'd come there. Police Chief Talbot led the others to the area where I'd found the second body.

Blake patted an anxious Treacle as I described how I had seen Samantha's bright hair.

Jake asked, "And you haven't moved the body?"

"No," I said. "Didn't even touch it."

Blake asked, "And you didn't notice anything else unusual?"

"You mean, aside from the skeleton?" I asked.

"Did you see any other evidence?"

I looked around. What they saw was what I did. Then I understood the intention behind his question and glowered at him.

"Well," Blake said, "you do steal evidence. You've done that."

"That was one time!" I said. "And what's important is that I didn't do anything like that this time. Cut me some slack, Samberg."

Jake interrupted with, "Blake, let's focus on the examination."

I watched Marlene examine Samantha's corpse until I felt queasy and had to turn away.

"Hmm," Marlene said, "all of this bruising is post-mortem. All of it."

I looked back, horrified, at the mottled gray and blue bruises on Samantha's arms, legs, and stomach. "I don't get it. Who would bruise her after she died? *How* did she die?"

I turned toward Jake and saw that the blood had drained from his face. Until recently, Bea's husband, Jake, didn't know our secret. He found out when he took on the case regarding Ted's death at the Brew-Ha-Ha.

Marlene looked up. "We'll need a more detailed autopsy. Cause of death might have been something like poison, but from what I can see so far, it wasn't physical trauma."

"Look at this—" Blake noted a strap of leather in Samantha's hand, frayed at the edge as if it had snapped. It was part of a dog's leash.

"Oh, poor thing," I whispered. At Blake's quizzical expression, I explained, "On the way here, over at the bridge, I saw this giant St. Bernard with a broken bit of leash on the collar…"

At that moment, Diane Davis, the newest member of the Wonder Falls police force, walked over. "We've found an open grave that the other body might have belonged to."

The three of us followed Diane to a crater in the ground, or more like a narrow tunnel. The tunnel's mouth was irregularly shaped and surrounded by loam and chunks of what might have been the grave marker.

Diane reported, "Boone took a look at the other body. Some parts were over fifty years old."

"Only some parts?" I asked.

Diane nodded. "A body that old shouldn't still have decomposing gristle on it."

"That's strange." Blake pointed at the grave. "And that's strange. If I were digging up a corpse,

I would shovel the dirt out of the way. From how the earth is scattered evenly around it, the grave looks like it was broken from below."

I spared a glance at Jake, who, if possible, turned even paler.

"Maybe an explosive," Blake guessed. "Buried and remote-controlled. We ought to check for shrapnel in the ground. Once the coffin top was broken, a grave-robber only needed to fish for it, lift the bones out, without disturbing the earth… no fingerprints on the casket…"

Jake might know our secret now, but he didn't like to talk about it. Maybe it was his way of pretending that none of it was real. But as I watched him grow paler and paler, I could only guess that he had concluded that the skeleton had come alive with some dark magic and clawed its way out of the grave.

"I think I'll go pack up my blanket now." With another glance at Jake, I added, "I'll be with Astrid and Bea at the Brew-Ha-Ha."

"Good," Jake said faintly.

"When's it opening again?" Diane asked. "Coffee and sodas just fail as a pick-me-up compared to Astrid's herbal mixes."

"Renovations are almost done," I said.

But with these new revelations, the renovations might just have to wait a little longer.

4. Resurrection Spell

A unt Astrid spotted me coming into the Brew-Ha-Ha. "Cath! You're back!"

"And you're early," Bea added. She craned her neck over the mezzanine railing and noticed the other guest. "Hello there, Treacle!"

"I *am* early." I sighed. "I found something awful at the graveyard."

Aunt Astrid set the paintbrushes to soak in their cleansers and sealed the tin buckets of varnish. She led Bea and me down the trapdoor behind the bar and into her nuclear bunker.

The last time I'd been in here, it had just been a dusty room with cement walls and a single flashlight. Now, it had been wallpapered and furnished with a low oval table and beanbag chairs, and she'd added some decent lights in paper-and-wire lampshades to make it seem more like a cozy secret place than a panic room. The trapdoor had been edged in something rubbery that made it difficult to close behind me.

"That's for soundproofing," Aunt Astrid said proudly when she saw me struggle with the door.

"Nice," I said.

"I stocked the mini-fridge," Bea said on her way down the stairs. "Everything here is being powered by the solar panels we put on the roof, but we also have a gas generator, although we should remember to change that every so often. Gasoline expires fast. Oh, and I opted for tatami over carpeting because of the way most carpeting catches mold spores and dust, but I did get a carpet-covered scratching post!"

Treacle made for the corner where the scratching post was and began to claw at it while the three of us settled down. I caught them up on what had happened.

Bea's first reaction was to shake her head sadly. "Poor Samantha!"

"Does she deserve so much of our pity though?" Aunt Astrid wondered.

"Mom!" Bea exclaimed, shocked. "Empathy isn't something that another human being has to deserve, especially when they've died."

"You're entitled to pity that she's dead," Aunt Astrid reassured her. "What I'm wondering is if she brought it on herself. We've had to deal with people trying to use magic for their own selfish reasons before, and we rescued them from taking on more than they could handle. Such arrogance can hurt and kill others in the process."

"It sounds to me like a resurrection spell gone wrong," Bea said. "But what if Samantha wasn't looking to be queen of the zombie armies?"

"You might be right," I said. "Samantha could have been the human sacrifice needed to resurrect another person."

"Even if Samantha Perry did it herself, with good intentions or ill intentions at heart," Aunt Astrid said, "we should find out *how* that much was accomplished and *why* it didn't work."

Bea nodded and asked me, "Who was it that came back to life? Maybe there's some connection between them."

"I don't know. The headstone was shattered. We'd better just let the officers investigate for now. If they find any evidence of a third person there, or put the headstone back together or something, you would know. Jake would tell you about it first, Bea."

Bea gave a sad laugh. "Oh, I don't know about that. Jake never wants to talk about magic with me."

"Poor man," Aunt Astrid said soothingly. "After last time, I'm sure it's just shock. Don't worry, Bea. He'll talk because he needs us to know."

"And we need him," I added.

Bea nodded again. "If or when it gets unbearable to pretend that Jake and I are normal and happy, like we used to be, well... can I please stay at either of your places?"

"In a heartbeat," I told her.

"As if you have to ask!" Aunt Astrid exclaimed.

I was convinced it would never come to that. At least, I really hoped it wouldn't. We hugged it all out and went back to varnishing the mezzanine, this time with my help. Min had had to leave to help his family at their store.

Treacle also went off, wandering into town. I'd long since learned that there was no stopping him at the best of times.

5. Shelley Marina

I mulled over possibilities the whole day. When I got back home that evening, I took too long in the shower and came out to find that I'd missed over a dozen calls on my cell phone from Blake. Or Detective Samberg, as I should really be calling him. We were friends, sort of, except when I hated him.

I called him back. "What's so—"

He interrupted. "Shelley Marina, 1878 to 1958. Do you know her?"

I scrambled to understand who he meant. "That was the name and date on the tombstone that got blown up?"

"Yes. We put the pieces together. Only literally."

"How could—"

"We still have metaphorical pieces. The case is still unsolved."

"I think I got that, Blake. I don't know her. She died before I was born."

"Could you find out anything about her?"

I hoped so. I wouldn't let on that I was investigating though. "No offense, Blake, but that's your job and not mine."

He paused. "Have I said or done something recently to make you angry?"

Angry wasn't the word. "Look, I just came across something really awful today and..."

"Oh, really? What was it?"

Was the man being sarcastic or utterly clueless?

My expression couldn't show over the phone, but I was sure it conveyed equal parts confusion, outrage, and self-disdain. Why was I surprised? I should really have known Blake better by now. Although I really shouldn't call him that. He was Detective Samberg. And the things he said were just Detective Samberg being Detective Samberg.

I hung up. The man was so incapable of human empathy that it wasn't even funny.

Bea laughed when I told her about my conversation with Blake the next morning. Seeing that I wasn't pleased, she covered her mouth with her hand to stifle the laughter.

"I think he's socially autistic," I said.

"Let's be more quiet," she whispered. "Aunt Astrid's in the bunker, doing her thing to find, you know, tangents." We were in the restaurant area of the Brew-Ha-Ha.

Tangent was the word Bea and I had made up to refer to people who might be witches and not know it. Tangents could see into the other world and usually thought that they were hallucinating or, if they were old, getting senile. Tangents could even make things happen with magic, only they wouldn't know about the facts and history behind their magic because they wouldn't know that they were part of a lineage of witches and wizards.

"I thought the bunker was soundproof," I said. "Why do we have to be quiet?"

Bea shrugged and sifted through one of Aunt Astrid's dozens of notebooks on the floor, the contents handwritten. "We still don't want to be too loud and disturb whatever we might disturb."

Min whispered as he edged between us. "What's disturbing?"

I jumped and yelped in surprise.

"What?" Min asked. "It's just me! You never used to be so jumpy."

I almost answered that I wasn't so careful about my family's secret when we were teenagers. I'd still taken care, of course, because I knew it was important. Now that I was older, I knew just how much was at stake if our secret ever got out.

So instead, I answered, "Yesterday gave me a bad turn."

"Oh, yeah." Min flinched. "I heard about Samantha. When did this town get so dangerous?"

I thought that it was a crime, not a natural disaster, so it wasn't a matter of when. Somebody had made my town dangerous, and I was going to track them down. That was probably the attitude that Blake expected me to take the night before.

Bea explained to me, "Min thought that he'd help a little more today with the renovations, but Mom's got it in her head that she dreamed of Samantha Perry's death before, and if she could only remember the details, then the police could track down the culprit. I told Min that she's meditating right now."

The town knew Aunt Astrid as a fortune teller. It was strange. Humans believed in magical abilities up to a certain point. After that point, they found it entirely inconceivable and terrifying.

Aunt Astrid had a better memory of her visions of the future if they came to her when she was awake. She only wrote down the dreams that felt like they could come true, but she always forgot the dreams after writing them down.

"I'd help with going through the notebooks, but I can't read your aunt's handwriting," Min said.

"Neither can I," I lied, squinting at the pages. "And this is still Aunt Astrid's café, so she gets to direct how everything gets rebuilt. It's better to wait for her to get convinced that she's done all she could do." I shrugged. "Sorry, Min, I guess there's not much to do here after all."

"I could still hang around," Min said hopefully. "I don't really have any other friends in Wonder Falls, and I remember what you said, Cath, about nobody really wanting a white knight entrepreneur."

Bea and I exchanged glances. I liked having Min around, but he couldn't learn the Greenstone secret. It was hard enough for Bea and Jake, and they were already married.

"Actually," Bea said, getting up and moving over to the bar, where she'd left her bag. "It depends on the industry you're in. My friend, Naomi LaChance, manages this theater troupe—"

"The Curtains?" I asked.

Bea took a business card out of her purse pocket. "Here it is! Of course, The Curtains, Cath. Naomi doesn't run any other troupe for the local community theater."

"But they're terrible!" I exclaimed.

Bea pouted at me. "They do their best."

"They staged *Norma* for their autumn show last year," I said to Min. "I think only two people had had voice lessons and none for opera. Nobody in the audience understood Italian. I don't think that even was Italian—" I did want to keep the family secret, but sending him off to invest in a void of talent would be too harsh.

Min took that all in and came to entirely the wrong conclusion. His face broke into a smile. "It sounds like they need a lot of help!" He took the card from Bea.

I acknowledged, "They wouldn't turn down a patron, but it really shows that they've got contradictory artistic visions. Everybody has huge egos—"

"I can manage egos," Min said confidently.

"Naomi LaChance would be overseeing rehearsals right now," Bea said to him, pointing. "At the address on the card."

"Thanks!"

Nobody was listening to my warnings. Granted, I didn't even know what the Curtains would be up to this year. I hope it wouldn't be nearly as terrible.

"I'll be back soon," Min said.

Bea sighed. "Oh, take your time. This"—she waved at Aunt Astrid's dream diaries—"will definitely take a lot of ours."

Just as suddenly as he'd sidled up to us, Min was gone.

Bea and I sat on the floor around the notebooks and continued to sift through the text until the trapdoor behind the bar creaked open. Three cats came out. The first was Peanut Butter, Bea's dun-coated shorthair Abyssinian. Peanut Butter was usually high-strung and nervous. This time he was high-strung and excited. He rubbed against Bea and *miaowed* as she patted his head.

"Is that so?" I said aloud, catching Peanut Butter's meaning behind the *miaow*. "No luck?"

"Oh yes," Aunt Astrid said as she emerged from the bunker and shut the trapdoor behind her. "We've eliminated a lot of possibilities, but…"

"But no tangents then," Bea summed up as she stood and dusted herself off.

Aunt Astrid shook her head sadly. "Not a one."

"It's about time these kittens learn their magic," came another thought from Aunt Astrid's cat, a longhaired white Maine Coon named Marshmallow. Marshmallow had been born looking like a grouchy grandmother, and at nine human years of age, she was finally beginning to act like one. *"But it wasn't a total waste."*

Aunt Astrid continued, "They would have Familiars in the other world, waiting to help train them."

I nodded.

"There are rules that tangents must follow," Aunt Astrid continued. "Firm rules. Even if they don't know them."

"I had no idea that the other world was so political," I said. "I thought that it was just strange and weird all the time."

"When it matters," Aunt Astrid said, "the Maid of the Mist can be very clear about what is allowed and what is not."

Peanut Butter sniffed at Aunt Astrid's notebooks and purred.

"He's worried about you and Jake," I translated. "Wow, Bea, how bad is it?"

"I don't know," Bea admitted. "Jake won't talk about it. He just said that he'll do what he can, and he trusts the Greenstones to do what we can."

Aunt Astrid gave Bea a comforting pat on the shoulder. "That sounds like a healthy boundary. Everyone needs that; we just forget it in a marriage."

"Boundaries? No, he's completely shut me out! Even Blake Samberg wants to talk more about the case to Cath."

I had a thought. "Shelley Marina was the resurrected. I don't suppose we could do a séance or something to ask her about why she came back to life?"

"That's not a talent that any of us have," Bea pointed out. That didn't make it impossible, but that would make it difficult. We risked burning out on magical energy if we did something too far outside of our talents.

Aunt Astrid added, "If we relied on a ritual, the biggest help would be a waxing moon—and the moon was full last night."

Silence hung in the air as we processed that.

"If…" I began. "If whoever did this wants to try this resurrection spell again, and isn't even a natural witch or wizard, would they need the full moon again?"

Aunt Astrid considered that. "I'm not sure. Magic is more of an art than a science. Whoever's done this might have discovered a different way to do it than our way because, of course, we keep our ways secret."

"But I studied other ways to heal," Bea said. "There are all sorts of different ways to do spells for the same outcome. The moon really affects certain spells we do. I think it's likely it would be a factor in someone else's spells too."

"So we wait." I groaned in defeat and leaned back until I was lying on the floor. Treacle climbed up on my stomach and lay on it as if he were an Egyptian sphinx.

6. The Wake

A week and a half later, I attended Samantha Perry's memorial service. Judging by the turnout, she'd been popular among the townspeople, especially the young rebels, but Samantha didn't have family in town. She'd only moved to Wonder Falls three years ago. That made it hard for Jake's investigation.

I knew that because I saw and talked to Jake there. I also thought that he had some explaining to do in regards to Bea. I didn't want to start a fight at a funeral, but I was really bad at masking my annoyance.

As mourners milled about on the lawn in front of the church, I went up to Jake and said, "You're all in black. This isn't official duty then?"

"Yes and no," he answered. "Plainclothes should still be appropriate for the occasion."

"I thought Bea would be with you."

Jake looked surprised. "She couldn't come with me. She had…" He looked around at the mourners, as if to check that nobody was listening, then added in a low voice, "Some investigating to do with this case."

"It's so obvious what you're doing." I shook my head. "Jake, investigating this case is why I'm here. I checked the guest book, and nobody has the surname of Marina or Perry."

He cleared his throat and walked, signaling me to follow. I did.

Jake asked, "You tried to find a connection that way?"

"We're out of options on the magic investigation side. We really have no clue."

"Don't say that, please."

"But it's true."

"You can tell me the truth, just don't use the M-word."

I rolled my eyes.

Oblivious, Jake continued, "How can you be out of options and not have a clue? Don't you have—"

"The thing I'm not even supposed to say that we have?" I asked. "Does Bea have to talk around this, just like what we're doing now? Never mind answering that. I know the answer. The point is, it's more complicated than that, but we've done our best and turned up with nothing."

"You weren't going to find Marina on the guest book," Jake muttered. "If she had a daughter, Marina would have become a maiden name. In some places, the government still uses the mother's maiden name as a special evaluator for sensitive information."

"I know that," I said crossly.

"I thought you might, but I wasn't sure. Changing last names doesn't seem to be Greenstone tradition."

"It isn't."

"So did Bea get in trouble with your aunt when she wanted to become Bea Williams?"

"You could ask her yourself," I answered primly.

Jake's shoulders slumped. "Right."

I felt sorry enough for him that I added, "Aunt Astrid and I support Bea with everything, but the Greenstones have a legacy tied to the name. Bea gave that up for you."

"I don't want anything done for me," Jake grumbled. "I wish this was a part of her life that she could do with me, both of us together."

"Magic—"

"Ugh!"

"The thing," I said, "doesn't work like that, especially if you don't even want to use the word! It's usually bad news when people who aren't witches try to do the thing."

"Can we not use the W-word either?"

"I don't need to use the W-word if I turn you into a toad for being annoying and hurtful." I did not have the ability to do that, but Jake's expression looked cautious.

He said, "I'm not hurtful. I'm just over-whelmed by things too strange to handle."

"Welcome to the witch world. Peanut Butter thinks you're getting a divorce, and it's making him more anxious than usual. I share a heart and mind sometimes with animals, so that's been making me more anxious than usual. Also, Bea's been getting depressed, and I care. So should you! So I'm sorry that you're overwhelmed, but you can't honestly tell me that you're not also being hurtful." I realized that we were getting close to the low stone wall that was the other entrance to the graveyard. "Where are we going?"

"Blake found Samantha Perry's dog when we got here, and he ran into the woods after the dog. I'll call him to say that the wake's about to start." Jake got his phone out and dialed. He paused. "Why do we call it a wake?"

I assured him, "It has nothing to do with Samantha waking up after being dead." The poor dog had been without Samantha to take care of it for days, I thought.

"Blake," Jake spoke into his phone, "I'm with Cath Greenstone. We're waiting for you at the back entrance." He paused. "You took the dog to the animal shelter? All right." He ended the call. "It sounds like we have our first witness in custody."

I blinked. "I thought you were talking to Blake about a dog."

"Cath," Jake said, "I'm trying to be more open about this. Didn't you just say that you could talk to animals?"

The realization dawned on me. "I don't speak Dog very well, but it's worth a try."

7. Burger

J ake drove us to the animal shelter. The place was comprised of mostly chicken-wire enclosures with corrugated tin roofs where animals of the same species could run free. There was one tiny tiled room that served as a vet's office and was also where the mammals could be bathed. In the lobby was a long sofa of scratched-up, worn leather. I knew the place well, since I volunteered there a couple of times a month. Old Murray waited in the lobby with an unconscious Blake Samberg stretched out on the sofa.

"How did you get him to sleep?" Jake asked Old Murray.

Murray mustered up a sad smile. "I've had a lot of practice. You get as old as me, with friends who are as old as I am, and you've got to learn to handle them when their minds start going."

I peered at the gray half circles under Blake's eyes. I whispered, "Has he really not slept since Samantha's murder?"

"Of course he has," Jake whispered. "It would kill him otherwise. But every time he wakes up, Blake gets angry with himself for taking that time out of the case to sleep. He'll keep working until he faints. Then he technically sleeps, once he's fainted, but he has nightmares that he's solved the case, and the nightmares wake him up, and his epiphany makes no sense. He just won't accept that the Perry case could remain unsolved."

"He rambles a lot," Old Murray agreed. "He said the dog was evidence, but he couldn't take it to the police station because of conspirators."

"Conspirators? Blake must be paranoid..." I sighed then turned to Old Murray. "Can we see the dog that Blake brought in?"

Old Murray looked from me to Jake. "I told Cody to give the dog a bath." Murray looked worried. "Could the dog really have evidence on her? I kept the collar, if you want to look at it."

"I'll examine the collar," Jake said decisively.

"And I'll help Cody bathe the dog," I said. "I mean, she's a big dog."

As Old Murray wandered off to get the dog collar, Jake went with me to the tiled room. Old

Murray had told me before that Blake volunteered frequently when there wasn't a case going on. I'd never run into Blake at the animal shelter though.

All of the veterinary equipment had been moved into the hall, on top of the stainless steel examiner's table. I knocked on the door to the tiled room and waved through the square window at Cody, who strained to reach over and turn off the faucet.

"Can I help?" I called through the window.

Cody looked me up and down—of course, I'd dressed for Samantha's memorial service, not for this—and said, "Nah, I'm fine. There isn't room."

The dog began to growl.

Jake asked, "Cath, what's happening?"

"I don't need to get in there to ask what's so wrong," I answered. "I can do it from here—"

That was a mistake. I reached out with my mind and got a single terrified and angry idea shot back at me. The dog lunged at the door, knocking Cody to the ground, its teeth bared in a snarl.

"Cody!" I shouted.

Jake threw himself between the door and me. His body slammed the door shut as the dog's muzzle tried to pry it open. "Cath, get out of here!"

I stood there, stunned.

"It's you!" Jake shouted. "Whatever you tried to do made the dog go wild! Just get out of here!"

I backed away and ran down the hall, out of the animal shelter, and into the driveway, where I caught my breath and tried to make sense of what had just happened. Jake followed a few minutes later, carrying the dog's collar. Old Murray and a limping, suds-covered Cody waved him farewell.

"We're not taking Blake with us?" I asked.

"He needs his rest," Jake answered. "Can you explain to me what just happened?"

I already knew some of the basics from experience and intuition. I would need to catch Jake up on that first. The truth was, I couldn't make complete sense of what had happened at the animal shelter. I took the collar, got in the car's front passenger seat, and Jake started driving. I saw from the tag that Samantha's dog was named Burger.

"It was like Burger was afraid of magic," I told Jake. "Most animals I talk to don't notice that what I'm doing is magic at all, because the mind and heart are part of instincts—senses that animals use all the time. They might be surprised that a human can talk to them the way that I do, but they don't think so much about it that they can't believe it while it's happening. That's a human thing. Some creatures, like fish or something, I can take over their minds completely because their minds are simple enough. People are too complicated, especially the ones that think about thinking. Domestic animals can be somewhere in between, and I guess Burger had a viewpoint that recognized magic and rejected it."

"Because Burger saw the magic happening," Jake concluded.

"It must have been the darkest magic, and it took Burger's only companion away from her. But it makes no sense! Aunt Astrid did a search for natural witches who didn't know that they were witches, and that turned up nothing. So that means that whatever happened to Samantha didn't come from a witch's talent. Burger shouldn't have recognized it as the same kind of magic."

"But it's both magic," Jake pointed out.

"There's a difference between music and noise, but both are sounds," I explained. "A ritual from a non-witch or wizard would have a specific feel. Magic that comes from a talent has a more natural feel, closer to reality."

"But it's all magic," Jake repeated. "It killed someone who's supposed to be alive, brought someone back to life who was supposed to be dead, and influenced a giant dog to attack you. Is there anything else I should know about how dangerous this is?"

There was a lot more to magic than what Jake knew, and they weren't all bad things. I wasn't in a mood to reassure him anymore though. "Magic killed my parents. It opened a portal to another dimension, and something unfriendly that had never been human came through. My dad was a non-witch who didn't stand a chance, and my mom was a witch who could only just manage to save me." That was all true, but I went on sarcastically. "Magic is barely a solution to the problems that we only have because of magic."

Jake drove on in silence and dropped me off at my house, where Treacle was waiting for once. I changed out of my black dress and into something more casual for the rest of the day, and I caught Treacle up on what I'd discovered.

Treacle had a lot of disdain for dogs and informed me that Marshmallow wanted the both of us to stay over at Aunt Astrid's place. I gave Aunt Astrid a call, and she told me to come right on over.

8. Unfamiliars

"An animal afraid of your magic?" Aunt Astrid pondered that as she set the dining table for three. In the kitchen was enough macaroni and cheese—more like penne and fondue cheese with cayenne pepper—for five people. "Our whole lives dedicated to witchcraft, and we're still learning something new every day."

I gave a humorless laugh as I set down water dishes for Marshmallow and Treacle. "If you think that's bad, I should tell you that Jake learned more about magic today than he ever wanted to know. I wonder if whoever—whatever—tried to do the resurrection might not even have been a person."

I went to the kitchen to wash my hands. When I came back into the dining room, Aunt Astrid was still thinking about it.

"The Unfamiliar," she said, which was what we called the beings from the other worlds who weren't helpful.

That was also what we called beings that we hadn't decided would be helpful or unhelpful. When it came to Unfamiliars, we witches were kind of like kids who are taught not to talk to strangers. We just didn't know how dangerous an Unfamiliar could be, and the safest thing to do was to not have any association with them.

"The worst ones would know how to get past the notice of the Maid of the Mist," Astrid said. "They would be a pure expression of talent, enough to spook poor dear Burger. To do that kind of thing, they would need the vessel of a human."

I nodded. "Would an Unfamiliar really risk getting Samantha killed? Especially for a human that was definitely dead?"

"We would have noticed if Samantha was being used as a vessel."

That was true. Unfamiliars needed to familiarize themselves with their targets so that they could move from their world and into ours. Their attempts would be like hauntings, possessions—something that witches couldn't miss, even if the unfamiliar could get past great beings like the Maid of the Mist.

"Maybe this Unfamiliar made a grave mistake—literally," I suggested. "Maybe it did make Samantha its vessel but got her to do something that accidentally killed her. The Unfamiliar probably got kicked out of Samantha's body after that happened."

"We need to make sure of that before we relax and mourn the unlucky Samantha Perry," Aunt Astrid told me. "But I think of the timing and the act—it's too human. It was as if it were motivated."

"The Unfamiliar have motivations too, I'm sure," I said. "It's just that they never explain or express themselves properly."

"Understatement of a lifetime!" Aunt Astrid exclaimed.

"The Unfamiliars just aren't reasonable," I concluded.

Aunt Astrid set out the bottle of chilled white wine and said, "Won't you get the door?"

I had already made my way to the front door and turned the doorknob before I realized that there had been no knock, no doorbell ring. Bea stood at the doorstep with Peanut Butter in one arm and a trolley-bag in the other. She looked as if she'd been crying.

"Jake did not just kick my cousin and soul-sister out of her own home," I said, mostly to myself.

Bea shook her head and sniffled. "Jake said that he needed some time apart to think about things. I needed to leave. This is my home, with you and Mom and all of our cats."

I let her in, and we all dined on Bea's favorite comfort food and got slightly drunk on her favorite wine. Even though Bea insisted that Jake's need to take a breather was not my fault at all, I volunteered to make a run for the chocolates and DVD rentals Bea loved.

Change is another part of life. Life itself goes on, even when we feel like it shouldn't. Some things are so awful that the whole planet should stop and turn its face back to just notice. It never does, not even for witches.

I wanted to contact the spirit of Shelley Marina, but Aunt Astrid informed me that it would do no good, since Shelley was so old. Contacting Samantha Perry, Aunt Astrid was certain, wouldn't go well either, since Samantha would be too confused and upset this soon after death to be a good witness. Contacting the dead was no easy feat.

During the day, the three of us continued to work on the Brew-Ha-Ha. We moved in new tables and chairs, stocked up on new cups and glasses and saucers. While we were restocking, Min came back.

"The place looks great!" he said as he shook his umbrella dry and left it open on the patio. He stomped his shoes dry on the doormat.

Aunt Astrid laughed. "Welcome back. You've missed a lot."

"So have we, by the looks of it. You're back to wearing business suits, Min," I remarked.

"I'm a producer now, for the Curtains' next show. I wanted to personally issue my favorite family in town…" He gave a dramatic pause and drew a stack of cards from his pocket before finishing. "Their complimentary tickets!"

"Four of them," Bea observed, with a little smile that I knew was hiding a pang.

"For Jake, of course." In the silence that followed, Min's joy visibly wilted. "What did I say?"

"Excuse me," Bea said softly, heading behind the bar and into the bunker.

Even Aunt Astrid didn't know what to say.

"Nothing wrong, it was really thoughtful," I said to Min and flinched. "It's just that, as Aunt Astrid said, you've really missed a lot."

"What's wrong with Bea and Jake?" Min asked, sitting at one of our new tables.

I couldn't tell him the truth. "That's between them."

"We just support Bea emotionally through it all," Aunt Astrid agreed. "Want a cup of hot tea or coffee?"

"This might be hot chocolate weather," Min said hopefully.

"I'll get right to that," Aunt Astrid said with a smile and flicked her gaze from me to the table.

I sat down.

Min spoke first. "If you don't know what's going on between them, then why do you look like you blame yourself for it?"

"I've got resting guilt face. It doesn't mean anything," I lied.

"Cath!" Min exclaimed. "What happened to us?"

"Us?"

"You, me, and Bea. We were like the three Musketeers, except that we actually used muskets."

"Those were toys," I pointed out, but I understood what he was saying. "Bea and Jake have a problem that they don't even want to talk to each other about. If they don't catch each other up on everything after making one of the most binding commitments of adult life, then what chance does a cousin have?"

"Cousin and soul-sister," Min reminded me.

I'd use that phrase so many times for Bea and myself that it had become second nature.

"Marriage," I mused. "Apparently it's complicated."

"My parents never talked as much to each other as I've heard was recommended," Min remarked. "I don't know if that's an Asian thing or a generational thing."

"Aunt Astrid and Uncle Eagle Eye talked about everything, but it only made any sense to the two of them. Flower children, you know." I remembered them together better than Bea did because I'd been old enough to remember when my uncle passed away. "My parents didn't talk a lot, but then again, I was at that age when my mom was still all about just being my mom."

"All marriages are different," Min concluded. "A big decision like Jake's doesn't just come up because a third person said this or that thing. It must have been going on for a while, so don't blame yourself."

That was also right. It didn't make me feel much better though.

Aunt Astrid brought hot cocoa for the three of us.

"Jake's uninvited to the show until he realizes what a treasure Bea Greenstone is," Min said to us.

Aunt Astrid and I cheered with our voices, then we cheered with our mugs clinking against each other.

9. Topher

Bea was enthusiastic enough about the show to let herself forget about Min's well-intentioned fourth ticket. At Aunt Astrid's insistence, we dressed formally, despite Bea's laughing objection that it was only the Curtains.

My objection, once I looked through Aunt Astrid's bedroom window at the moon in the afternoon sky, was more grim. "We should be ready to get to the graveyard and fight zombies tonight, shouldn't we?"

"No, that's a gibbous moon," Aunt Astrid corrected without looking up. "The full moon is tomorrow."

"Already?" Bea gasped. "Well, it could be that nothing will happen."

"And that would mean that Samantha Perry died for no reason that we could find," I grumbled.

Aunt Astrid sighed. "That happens too."

A car horn sounded from the driveway. I looked down to see a limousine and a familiar figure in a blazer. The three of us tottered out into the driveway on our spindly high heels, wearing glittering shawls.

"What's this about?" I called to Blake where he leaned against the limousine door.

"Security detail," he replied gruffly.

The tinted window of the front seat rolled down, revealing Officer Diane Davis in the driver's seat. Diane blared the car horn again, waved, and said, "We'll protect you!"

Behind me, Bea exhaled heavily. Maybe she had been hoping to see Jake and Blake, the not-so dynamic duo.

"You look nice," I told Blake. "You should get sleep more often."

He cleared his throat and gave me a quick once-over. "You look... not so bad yourself."

This was the closest thing to a compliment I'll ever get from Blake. He opened the passenger door and ushered the three of us in.

Mrs. Park was waiting inside, and she and Aunt Astrid greeted one another warmly. Mrs. Park was almost two decades younger than Aunt

Astrid, but she looked two decades older, especially that night, because of her nervousness.

"Mr. Park won't be joining us?" I wondered.

"Oh, no!" Mrs. Park exclaimed. "He thinks that the performing arts is a wasted career track and doesn't know why Min would invest in this show of all things."

Aunt Astrid clucked her tongue. "Min could invest in a wasted career track like this theater troupe four times a year for the rest of his life and still have enough for retirement. Isn't that right?"

"It is," Mrs. Park agreed. "And Min argued the same way. He should know his father by now, but I know he will be so disappointed when he sees that Mr. Park didn't change his mind."

"Well," I said wryly, "I've actually seen Mr. Park at a show staged by the Curtains, so he knows what Min's getting into."

"Don't be mean, Cath!" Bea exclaimed. "This is in honor of Tommy."

"The Curtains aren't without talent," I conceded. "It's just that they're so ambitious. Operas and ballets! Even their avant-garde stuff shows no concept of working within their limitations. I'm not even talking about the budget."

"I never met Thomas," Mrs. Park said. "Min looks up to him a lot now. It's funny."

I didn't think that was so strange. What I wondered was when Samantha would get anything grand done in her honor and what it would be. Then I wondered why Min would invite Blake. I thought they didn't get along.

We would soon find out.

Blake escorted the four of us into the lobby of the Wonder Falls ballet theater, which had lush carpets and sparkling chandeliers. Most other audience members had opted for full-formal attire.

"You were right after all," Bea said to Aunt Astrid while craning her neck. "We aren't overdressed. Oh, look, there's Naomi up on the dais."

I peered in the direction Bea was pointing and saw that Min Park was standing with Naomi.

"Well, let's all go and say hi," I urged the other five.

Naomi squeaked with excitement when she saw Bea approaching. They gave each other a quick embrace and air kisses, then went to the side to chat. Min embraced his mother, nodded in greeting to Aunt Astrid, gave me a smile—and signaled at Blake to follow him.

"What was that about?" I asked nobody in particular.

"Security matters," Aunt Astrid guessed. "Maybe some of our less-than-model fellow townspeople haven't forgiven Tommy for that political article and are prepared to be less than constructive about it."

"That must be it," I said, completely convinced that it couldn't be it. "I'm just going to go make sure…"

I followed Blake and Min to an empty corridor, where of course I couldn't stay hidden until they made a turn. A set of double doors down the hall led to a function room, but I wouldn't be able to see or hear anything if I hid there. I ran forward as quietly as I could in heels but kept myself hidden behind the bend in the corridor. Blake was murmuring, and I heard, to my surprise, Old Murray's voice objecting.

"And here I thought you'd talk sense," Old Murray said to Blake. "Here's Topher's ticket, right here. It's his ticket, but it was mailed to my address. Now are you going to show us to our seats?"

"But you didn't reserve or confirm a seat for yourself," Blake said.

"You saw all I've got to do, Blake! Do you really want to see how Topher gets without me? It'd be better to leave both of us out of this show if that were to happen."

Then Min spoke up. "Topher is Tommy's only family, that's all I knew. I didn't know that he—"

A fourth voice, doleful and trembling with age, yelled, "Alice! I know what you did to my Alice!"

"Wasn't lucid," Min finished.

Old Murray told Topher to be quiet.

After a pause, Old Murray spoke again. "So did we come all this way for nothing? Or did you mean what you wrote about being honored to have Thomas's family watch the show? I'm his family too, you know. Tommy was my grand-nephew. My sister Dolores was a Willis before she became a Thompson."

"Dolores!" Topher's voice spoke again. "Don't leave us like this! She's left us, Murray."

"I know," Old Murray said to him. "I've known a long time. It's been a long time, Topher, think."

Blake and Min walked back up to the corner.

"We can wait for the theater to fill up and just count Murray's seat as a complementary walk-in, if there's room," Min said to Blake.

"Right," Blake said, "I'll notify the ushers." There was static like a communicator coming to life. "Davis, do you copy?"

Had this all been about seating arrangements? As Blake spoke instructions into his communicator, I risked peeking around the corner and gasped through my nose at what I saw. There was definitely something, a ripple in the air, over Old Murray's balding head. It was probably an Unfamiliar!

"I don't know if you can understand me," Min said to Topher, "but thank you for coming. Thomas was such an inspiration to all of us."

Topher lunged—lurched, more like, but feebly—toward Min. "You've got so much nerve to say that, to show your face here!"

Min's expression was one of confusion and hurt.

"Sit down, Topher," Old Murray said calmly—and there it was again, that ripple in the air that hurt my eyes.

When Topher sank to the floor, his wispy gray-and-white hair falling all over his face, I thought the Unfamiliar had succeeded in controlling Topher too. I ducked back around the corner.

Min almost stammered but quickly recovered the poise that he'd learned in his time away from

Wonder Falls. "I hope you don't mind waiting a little longer."

"Nah," Old Murray answered. "Although if you can get us any of those little sandwiches that they're passing around…"

"We'll do that."

Min's voice was too close. I tiptoed—in heels as high as the ones I wore, there was no other choice—down the hall, slipped into the function room, and pressed my ear against the door so that maybe I could catch what they were talking about as they passed.

Min asked, "Was that enough to confirm your suspicions?"

"No," Blake replied. "I can't deny my suspicions either, but I want to."

"Maybe we should have brought Cath in this time."

"We didn't have to," Blake said. "She brought herself."

"She what?" Min exclaimed.

The door I wasn't leaning on opened, and Min and Blake peered into the function room.

"How did you know I was listening?" I asked Blake.

"I'm a detective," he replied coldly. "I notice things."

They walked in, and Blake shut the door behind them.

"Old Murray Willis is my prime suspect," Blake explained. "I don't know how, because none of the evidence adds up to anything that makes sense, but Old Murray acted suspiciously and lacks an alibi. He had Cody bathe Burger when I told him that the dog was evidence. What do you think?"

It was really too bad that I knew that the crime had been committed by an Unfamiliar possessing Old Murray, but I couldn't tell either of them. "You can't arrest Old Murray on a hunch."

Blake shrugged. "We can interrogate him. With lack of evidence, a confession will do."

"With the way you interrogate," Min said to Blake, "I think that's too harsh. I would know, since you ripped me to pieces in that interrogation room."

"He did?" I asked Min. "When?"

"Doesn't matter now," Min muttered.

"You're still alive," Blake said. "Samantha Perry was brutalized and left for dead. No justice and no peace. For anybody."

"I'm a grown man, and I can take your interrogation methods," Min said. "Murray is the sole guardian of a minor—Cody. He's Topher's only friend. Topher lost his mind and is practically a hundred years old. This won't end well. Cath, am I wrong?"

"Unfortunately, no," I told him.

Blake's expression was usually a glower, so I didn't know how to describe the look he shot Min. He did say, sharply, "Cath and I spend at least one afternoon a week with Old Murray at the animal shelter. We know what good he's done. But if he's guilty of a murder in this town, we can't stand for it."

"I'm not telling either of you, or anybody, to stand for it," Min said, opening the door to the hall. "I just can't be around when you take any of your terrible options."

I sighed when the door swung shut behind Min. "Why did Topher Thompson accuse Min of doing something to Alice? Who's Alice?"

"Who knows? Topher knows, obviously, but good luck getting him to explain."

"Couldn't he get taken into custody too? I don't mean like an interrogation; he needs a doctor." I added to myself that Topher also needed some expert witches to look him over and check to see that he didn't catch Unfamiliar spirits from his only friend.

"We'll do what we can." Blake was out the door before I could ask who he meant by "we."

10. The Curtains Rise

I thought that I would be a few minutes late for the show, but Naomi was still talking on the stage.

Bea whispered as I passed her, "You missed Min's eulogy for Tommy. Naomi had a shorter one because she started crying. She's introducing us about the show now."

Naomi continued, "This ballet was inspired by a German essayist, Heine, who traced the origins of the Wilis to Slavic and Austrian culture. The fantasy that they fulfill is common to humanity, whether that would be grief over the lost potential of a young life ended too soon or vengeance for deception."

"What are we watching again?" I whispered.

"*Giselle* is the name of the show," Aunt Astrid replied, "but personally, I'm watching those two old men up in the balcony seats."

I turned to look where Aunt Astrid had pointed. Sure enough, there was Old Murray and Topher.

Bea said to me, "One of them was very rude and loud when Min got onstage. I don't think he's well."

I cleared my throat discreetly. "Did either of you see anything... Unfamiliar about them?"

"Very," Aunt Astrid murmured.

Bea added, "Yes, but I don't know which one. It might be both."

"They'll be taken in at the end of the show, but I think I know which one of those men it's attached to. If they try anything before then..." I hoped that either Bea or Aunt Astrid would have a plan.

Their silence showed that they didn't, and Mrs. Park slipped into her seat beside Aunt Astrid just as the house lights dimmed.

I couldn't get too engrossed with the show, but it wasn't as bad as I'd thought it would be. None of the performers could dance ballet with the boneless grace of a performance-standard dancer, but the costumes were splendid—so money could sometimes buy entertainment-worthy quality. Nobody was trying to sing, at least.

I could relate to the protective mother of the frail and waiflike main character, and my favorite character was the princess huntress. They reminded me of Aunt Astrid, Bea, and myself. That was, until the title character got into a love triangle with two jerks, one who always lied and the other who told the truth—and it turned out the latter was worse, because that truth gave the main character a heart attack that killed her.

Then the house lights came on for the intermission between the first and second act. Old Murray and Topher didn't leave their seats during intermission, so neither did the three of us.

"I can't believe I didn't notice it at the animal shelter," I said, about Old Murray's Unfamiliar. "Burger didn't notice it either. I wonder if the Unfamiliar just wasn't around that day."

"Don't stop noticing it now," Aunt Astrid advised.

"Maybe we should," Bea suggested. "If it knows that we've noticed it, then it might try something. There are too many people here."

"Not right now," I whispered. "It's intermission."

Aunt Astrid shook her head. "They're too far away. There's no way to reach them from here with magic."

"If the abilities of the hosts are limited," Bea murmured, "the Unfamilars would be limited too."

I nodded. "Yes. They're already limited by human motivations and rules for performing spells under the full moon. The Unfamiliar would need to do a lot of work to get their host to do something improvised and magical. At least, I hope that's the case for these ones."

That had seemed to be the way it worked for the Unfamiliar that had haunted me and that had cost my parents their lives. The problem with the Unfamiliars was that we really would never know how they operated.

We had a tense evening, full of wary anticipation. It occurred to me that the Unfamiliar could take action even today. The gibbous moon could be mistaken for full. What if the Unfamiliar or its host decided that it was close enough? Something had gone wrong with the first resurrection spell. The collateral damage of approximations didn't come off as too much of a bother for this Unfamiliar.

"I wish that we could just tell the Maid of the Mist," I said. "You would think that she'd want to know. Hasn't she interfered before for less important things?"

"Less important to us," Bea pointed out. "She might be Familiar, but she must have different priorities that we can't understand. We might be a mystery to her too."

"We can agree that Unfamiliars like this are bad though, right?"

"That's right," Aunt Astrid said firmly. "What to do about it is up to witches."

"Not right now, it isn't," I said ruefully, as the audience members returned and the house lights dimmed for the second act.

Mrs. Park returned with small dumplings on toothpicks for the three of us, which I was sure wasn't allowed, but she was the producer's mother. All the tension was making me hungry. I ate too fast and hiccupped most of the way through the second act.

The main character came back from the grave to face down the queen of the ghosts of women scorned, and in doing so, she rescued the people who had killed her—or one of them. The choreographer must have taken liberties with the original choreography, because I thought we had come to see a ballet. The final dance turned into a collective tap like Riverdance, followed by more modern street dancing.

"What am I even watching right now?" I mumbled, flabbergasted.

"Watch your manners around Tommy's family," Aunt Astrid said, only because Mrs. Park was sitting with us. She meant that I should keep watching Old Murray and Topher.

It was a good thing she pointed it out, because I saw Topher stand up and disappear through the curtain behind his balcony seat. Old Murray followed him.

"I've got to be rude and walk out on this," I said to Bea. "And I might need to run after someone. I won't take my shoes with me."

"I'll find a way to explain it to Min and Naomi," Bea said.

I shrugged and smiled at Mrs. Park's gaze of disapproval. She always thought that I was too harsh and judgmental. For now, that would be my cover story.

11. The Escape

As I made my way up the aisle, I tried to remember the spell to pull a host apart from an Unfamiliar. The process was often one long and exhausting fight. Being a witch wasn't like in the movies where they had unlimited power. If we used too much magic, we might get magic burnout, which was very depleting, and it might take days, weeks, or even months to recover.

As I'd mentioned, as a child, I had almost become a host for an Unfamiliar spirit. My mother tried to explain to me that I had the power to keep it away from myself, but I was too young and scared to really understand how. That was the easiest way to prevent becoming a host for an Unfamiliar though—and the best way. Maybe things would have gone differently if I'd done it on my own.

Maybe I could simply talk Old Murray into rejecting the Unfamiliar, but I doubted that would work. It hadn't work for me, and I'd already known the basics of magic and witchcraft. Talking someone through the Unfamiliar rejecting process left too much to chance, especially if they weren't witches.

So I had no other choice but to use magic. I could do a binding spell. The Unfamiliar wouldn't leave the host but simply be bound inside the host so it wouldn't do any harm. It sounded unpleasant, but what else could I do?

By the time I decided that, I was in the theater lobby. I caught Diane speaking into her communicator as she made her way up the grand staircase.

"Area clear," she finished then looked alarmed when I ran up to her.

"Not a chance," I told her. "Topher and Old Murray left the balcony seats a few seconds ago. Where would they be now?"

"The balcony leads straight to either the west wing or the east wing," Diane replied.

"Of course you've got backup watching both."

Diane shook her head. "Blake and I are doing a favor, private security just for tonight. Min told us to expect those two to make their way down here after the show, then Blake could read them their rights in private and take them in for questioning."

I groaned and started up the staircase. Diane followed me as I almost scolded, "Well, they're trying to dodge us by getting out earlier than that." When we reached the top of the grand staircase, I told Diane, "You and Blake block the east wing. I'll block the west, and we'll have them surrounded—but if you find them first, don't do anything to threaten them. Just stall them until I meet with you."

There was no time to wait for her answer. I ran ahead to the west wing. Fortunately, that was where I found the both of them.

Murray was grappling Topher and saying, "I can't let you go out on your own and disappear again! Come back with me and just calm down!"

"Stop it!" I said as I fixed my gaze on the ripple over Murray's and Topher's heads. "You can't control him, Murray. You don't have the right. I'll give you one chance to leave him alone."

I concentrated on him to do my spell.

Murray raised his hand, palm toward me, and I was struck with a paralyzing fatigue. The Unfamiliar laughed. My knees buckled, and my field of vision darkened even though I tried desperately to remain standing and alert. In my panic, I thought I might have done the spell wrong.

But I sensed the Unfamiliar spirit's fading laughter. I used all of my strength to conjure a magic lasso. I made it wrap around the Unfamiliar again and again before tying a knot.

It had worked. For now. The spell could last a day, up to two or three, until I, or another witch, had to do it again. It took a lot of energy, and it wasn't sustainable for the long run.

Somewhere down the hall, footsteps sounded, followed by a scuffling sound. Murray made a grab for me as I began to faint.

A voice pulled my attention back to the world of the non-witches. "Step away from her! I'm telling you, I'm armed."

It was Blake. My vision focused, and I saw Old Murray looking confused and shocked.

Murray let me go. "What's going on here?"

Blake holstered his gun and drew a pair of handcuffs instead.

"I'm so sorry, Murray," I said as Blake snapped on the handcuffs.

Murray looked from his cuffed wrists, to Blake, to me, and back to his wrists. "What did I do wrong? I didn't do anything…"

He really hadn't, but there was no way to even try to tell non-witches what had really happened. Instead, I asked Blake, "Where's Topher?"

Blake nodded in the direction of farther down the hall. "I caught him as he was trying to run off and got him handcuffed. Diane will take care of him."

Diane trotted up behind him with her gun drawn. "Take care of what?" She saw us and holstered her gun.

Blake peered at her. "Wasn't there an old man in the hallway behind us?"

Diane paused. "Yes?"

Blake groaned with aggravation. "Diane! He was handcuffed and knocked out! Get back there and guard him like you were obviously supposed to!"

As Diane backed away apologetically, I raised an eyebrow at Blake.

"I can't wait until Jake clocks back in," Blake muttered.

"Handcuffed and knocked out? That's harsh, Blake. You could have given Topher a heart attack or a stroke." Old Murray, at least, was spry for his age, although I still felt sorry for him when he looked at us sadly. We took care of lost and injured animals together. We were friends.

Blake argued, "He attacked me first."

"He's over eighty years old! He couldn't have been too much of a threat."

As I said that, Diane jogged back into our hallway. She fidgeted a little and said apologetically, "The other old man got away. I went back and saw your extra handcuffs in the hall, so I tried to run him down—I guess he was faster than we gave him credit for."

"He was stronger too." Blake turned to Diane and said, "I think you should turn your resignation in to Chief Talbot."

Diane flinched. "That isn't fair, Samberg!"

I glared at Blake and touched Diane's shoulder. To Diane, I said, "Take us home first. Topher can't be all that difficult to find, right?" I looked at Blake, thinking that it would be on him to do it.

12. Normal

Diane drove us Greenstones and the Parks home.

"The first two-thirds, maybe, of the show wasn't all that bad," I admitted.

"If only Mr. Park had given the ballet a chance," Aunt Astrid said. "There's even a glowing review from Cath."

"Even if she did walk out." Bea chuckled.

Min talked about what had happened behind the scenes, the concepts that he enjoyed but didn't make it to the stage, and the battle of egos that I had warned him about.

We solved the mystery before the full moon, I thought. The town was safe again. I counted the binding spell on the Unfamiliar spirit as a victory, even if it is just for now.

There was still the question of how harsh the legal proceedings would be though. As uncompromising as Blake could be, I doubted that he would go too far in interrogating somebody who wasn't in their right mind and was so infirm of body. Maybe temporary insanity would be the best compromise between the truth and the consequences for Old Murray. I could only hope.

Bea was smiling again because she'd seen her friends. With some good old-fashioned family support, maybe she could figure something out with Jake.

Aunt Astrid and Mrs. Park had both been able to put on nice dresses and watch an entertaining show. Min had done something for the community like he wanted to.

We'd find Topher, or someone would, and we'd figure out a more reasonable explanation for his disappearance.

The Greenstones would finish renovating the Brew-Ha-Ha next week and have an opening party the day after.

Things were looking up.

Sometimes I wished I were normal. Then I remembered that not knowing about magic didn't stop it from ruining people's lives, and I realized that I was very lucky.

Then I forgot that and wished I were normal, because without magic, I'd have one less thing to think about on a crazy day.

The next morning got off to a running start. I received a call from the construction company's new accountant about a discrepancy in the amount billed for the Brew-Ha-Ha reparations. Something about the insurance, or the taxes, or the retainer fee—Bea usually did the numbers with that, so because the accountant was new and the filing was messy, I told them to call Bea. I gave them her house number, because it was the one I'd memorized. Then I realized only Jake lived there now. That wouldn't be so bad though. Jake was a good guy, and he would call Aunt Astrid to pass on the message, or even just give them Aunt Astrid's number instead.

Instead, I had my breakfast, got dressed, and received another call from the accountant about the Brew-Ha-Ha's internals manager no longer living at the number given.

"Is that what Jake is telling people?" I exclaimed, shocked and outraged. I might have called him some names, and I definitely hung up and stormed out.

On the walk to Bea and Jake's place—no, I thought with sarcastic fury, just Jake's place now—I checked my cell phone and found nine voice messages from Blake and two from Min. I'd expected the ones from Blake. Most of them were the increasingly improbable theories of a sleepless gumshoe, concerning Samantha Perry's murder. I wondered why he didn't just write them in his cop's notebook. I was more worried than flattered that he spent the entire night leaving me messages like that. The case was driving him nuts, and he didn't seem to have anyone else to turn to.

All right, maybe I was a little flattered—and a little frustrated, because I could never tell Blake anything close to the truth about these cases in Wonder Falls. The Greenstones had solved the Samantha Perry case, but we didn't have a cover story. An Unfamiliar took advantage of an aging man to stir up trouble in our physical world. How were we supposed to explain that? If not even Jake wanted to know, then Blake hadn't a hope.

According to Blake's messages, it had been Jake who convinced him to take up the security sideline at the show.

Blake's final message worried me the most. "No means, no motive, no evidence… this makes no sense. This makes no sense! This makes no sense! This makes no se—" He trailed off in wordless, muffled gargles of anguish. "Call me when you think of something."

Min's concerns were much simpler. His first message informed me that he wouldn't be available to help at the Brew-Ha-Ha because he had to talk something over with his dad. I winced. Min had always had a rocky relationship with his father. For Min's sake, I hoped that was water over the dam, but some family dramas never ended.

Min's second message informed me that he'd joined the search party to look for Topher.

The moment after I let all those messages play out, my phone buzzed to life with a call from Aunt Astrid.

"Honestly, Kitten Cath!" she exclaimed. "You have enough boy troubles of your own. You don't need to make more by interfering with Bea's."

I reached the corner of Rainfall and Riverfall and halted. Farther down Riverfall would take me to Jake's place, or I could turn the corner and head for Aunt Astrid's. Before making any decision, I needed to ask, "Aunt Astrid, how did you know that?" As far as I knew, Aunt Astrid could see the future, not the present.

Aunt Astrid answered, "Bea is helping me organize my dream journals. We're only a fraction of the way through, but I read some of my entries, and they…" She paused as if thinking of how to describe it. "They reminded me of the future."

"That might be helpful later, but don't we have more mundane problems to worry about?" I told her about the construction company.

"One moment—"

I listened to her distant voice speaking to Bea.

When I could hear Aunt Astrid properly again, she said, "Oh, dear."

I had mixed feelings then. Anger at Jake nagged my feet to run toward him. Worry nagged me to head for Aunt Astrid's house. Guilt kept me frozen to the spot.

Aunt Astrid said, "Leave Jake alone. Bea needs her family."

I bolted for Aunt Astrid's house.

13. Enough is Enough

The first thing I noticed when I stepped in the door was that the cats were on the table in the anteroom. Marshmallow was curled up like a large fuzzy dumpling. Peanut Butter was belly up, mouth open and panting.

"Peanut Butter!" I exclaimed. "What happened?"

"I told him," Marshmallow thought at me. *"I showed him the other world, the one we all share, where Bea heals. I told him he couldn't make worries go away or else the first one Bea would have healed was him!"*

"And Peanut Butter tried anyway," I guessed and tickled the tawny cat's belly.

Our cats could sometimes work magic. Marshmallow was the best at it, because Peanut Butter and Treacle were both too young. They sometimes managed it, when they joined together or used the help of their humans. To heal a human all alone though, without even knowing how... *"How bad is his burnout?"*

Marshmallow assured me, *"Peanut Butter doesn't need to go to the cat hospital."*

At that, Peanut Butter yowled. He sent me the thought, *"I'm fine! I want to try again to help Mommy. I need help."*

"I'm not helping you," Marshmallow grumbled, shifting so that she curled up into a smaller ball.

I sensed Peanut Butter calling for Treacle.

"Treacle's not here then," I said. He tended to be most feral of the three of them. Marshmallow was like a crochety old lady, and Peanut Butter was a scaredy-cat.

If Treacle wasn't at my place when I left and he wasn't here, then I wasn't sure where he was, and I wasn't surprised. Treacle also tended to worry much less about what he couldn't understand. When I realized that, I tried to comfort Peanut Butter with the thought that what made Bea upset was a human problem that we could solve without magic. Bea just needed Jake to quit being such a jerk.

"Treacle doesn't worry about what he doesn't understand," Marshmallow repeated my thoughts to me. *"We should both give him a stern talking-to. He*

won't attend our magic lessons! He thinks they're boring and we can always depend on our humans to do it!"

"The opposite problem you have with Peanut Butter then," I thought back.

"What am I going to do with these kittens? What are they going to do with themselves?" Marshmallow grumbled.

When I tried to pet Marshmallow between the ears, she lifted her head and nipped me.

Aunt Astrid was never as grouchy as Marshmallow could get. Bea could be sad but never seemed to reach the levels of desperation and anxiety that was Peanut Butter's personality. As I headed up the stairs to Bea's room, I thought about Treacle and decided to follow his example as a person of action… so to speak.

I knocked on the door to Bea's room, and Aunt Astrid let me in with a look of exacerbation. I saw Aunt Astrid's dream diaries stacked on one side of the room, forgotten, and I saw Bea lying belly-down on the bed as if she'd melted there. She lifted her head from the pillow, her eyes swollen as if she'd been crying.

"Enough is enough!" I announced. "Bea, I'm calling you a divorce lawyer!"

As Bea keened, "What? No!" I saw Aunt Astrid's expression shift from impressed to pretending to be shocked.

Aunt Astrid sat on the foot of Bea's bed. "Maybe I should have let you rip Jake a new one."

"Mom!" Bea exclaimed. "That's worse!"

"That," I declared, "is nothing. Maybe I said too much and scared Jake off from the Greenstones forever. But you know what? What I said was true. And what I said was... well, said!"

Bea looked confused.

"Because people are supposed to talk," I finished. "You and Jake are supposed to talk. He said he wanted space, time, peace, quiet—whatever. We should never have believed him! When his wife who loves him so much—who he's supposed to love back—is in this much pain, and he doesn't even know because neither of you will say anything to each other? He gets what he wants, but what I think we all need is balance. That means you get right in front of him, right now, upset and noisy! He can have his peace when there's nothing to ignore!"

Aunt Astrid applauded as Bea looked from me to her and back to me in disbelief.

"Cath, I..." She sounded as if she was going to cry again.

Aunt Astrid and I looked at each other. I couldn't usually read the minds of other human beings, but when it came to family, some things went without saying. We pulled Bea out of bed and pushed her into the bathroom. I rummaged through her bags of clothing, looking for sharp and intimidating outfits that she would never wear. Aunt Astrid looked through Bea's computer for the transaction records between the Brew-Ha-Ha and the construction company.

Aunt Astrid remarked, "Paper records, I know how to deal with. I have an awful feeling that Bea left them at Jake's."

About a half hour later, Bea emerged from the bathroom and said with more confidence, "I am not coming at Jake with a divorce lawyer."

Aunt Astrid heaved a sigh of disappointment, but I knew she didn't hate Jake or not want him in the family. That day, I hated Jake and wanted him out of Bea's life, but Aunt Astrid wasn't as impulsive as I was. But Aunt Astrid had been staying with Bea, living with her like this, and the magic didn't let Aunt Astrid have so much as a peek at the final solution.

"It's too sudden, too much for him, let alone me," Bea continued. Still, she stood up a little straighter. "But you're right, Cath. I'll give him a chance on more even terms. I'm going to talk to him."

She wouldn't wear the outfit that I chose for her though. She would go visit Jake, in all honesty, as the Bea he knew and loved.

At the door, we saw her off.

I asked, "Are you sure you don't want us to come with you?"

"I'm sure that's what you want," Bea said, but she laughed.

Aunt Astrid cleared her throat. "Well, the matter Jake has with you is a little offensive to our entire family legacy."

Bea assured us, "I can handle him on my own. Fair is fair is one on one."

I could tell that Bea was nervous though. Luckily, right then, I felt something brush my ankle and saw Peanut Butter between us. He looked at her with large amber eyes and gave a weak *miaow*.

I urged Bea, "At least take Peanut Butter with you!"

"I will," Bea said, bending down to pick up Peanut Butter. With his front paws on her shoulder and his hind legs cradled in her arms, Bea nodded good-bye at the both of us and set off for Jake's place.

Aunt Astrid shut the door. The look on her face was one of anticipating doom.

"At least Bea won't be alone," I said. Jake couldn't possibly feel ganged up on by one person and her pet.

Aunt Astrid remarked, as her expression changed to one of exaggerated innocence, "And you'll be able to check up on her through Peanut Butter."

I would never admit to that ploy ever having crossed my mind.

14. Burger's Bite

A unt Astrid and I sat down together to figure out what the problem was with the construction contractors' contract. I couldn't make heads or tails of it for the whole morning, although Aunt Astrid ultimately seemed to have figured out what had gone wrong. She made the call to their accountant while I made lunch: deli meat and cheese sandwiches, a giant garden salad, and some reheated crab-and-corn soup.

I let my mind wander to Treacle, letting our minds connect. *"I didn't leave food out for you,"* I reminded him. I used to do so, but that attracted other stray cats, and they tended to be rude or even violent to Treacle.

"That's all right," Treacle replied. *"I ate a field mouse on the way to the wire forest."*

That would be all right if it had only been words, but when I join my mind with animals, they spoke in ideas and feelings...and the full imagery of experience. I flinched when I sensed the crunch of field mouse bones, the smell of its urine, and the fleas tickling Treacle's whiskers.

"I wish you'd quit hunting wild things, Treacle. They could pass on worms in your gut that'll make you feel sick!"

"Some human foods for cats are poisoned," Treacle reminded me.

That had been a freak outbreak of contaminated pet food in China. I'd read a news report about it and translated it for Treacle, who took it entirely the wrong way.

"Some human foods for humans are poisonous too," Treacle thought. *"Life is always going to be dangerous."*

There was no convincing him otherwise. *"Marshmallow is grouchy that you don't take your magic lessons. Why did you go to the... wire forest?"* As I uncertainly repeated the thought back, I recognized the cracked concrete floor of the animal shelter—and the wire around the kennel area. Oh.

"Because," Treacle thought back at me triumphantly, *"I don't want to scare away our witness."*

The reply made no sense to me.

Through Treacle's eyes, I saw the edges of worn blue jeans and sneakers. Treacle looked up and miaowed at a figure too tall for me to recognize, until it stopped and sat down. The air took on a ragged quality as the human covered his face with his hands.

Cody, I realized. Cody Willis was crying. Of course he was. Old Murray was his grandfather, and the only family he had left. Old Murray had been arrested for a crime that he didn't commit.

There was nothing I could do.

"Cody? Are you all right?" said a familiar voice.

Cody wiped his tears away and tried to laugh. "That's what I've been asking you, Mr. Samberg."

Blake approached them both and petted Treacle on the head. "I know Old Murray can't have done it."

"How can we make everyone else know it?" Cody asked. "You have to prove it. We can't even prove how anybody could do the crime in the first place!"

Treacle trotted purposefully down the hall and into the yard.

"A witness," I thought, *"you don't want to scare away... what does that have to do with Marshmallow's magic lessons?"* Then I remembered Burger.

Samantha Perry's dog had been present when the crime took place, and she was afraid of magic. *"Treacle!"* I called urgently. *"Old Murray's been arrested! I feel sorry for Cody, but the mystery is solved. It's Old Murray, but it's not... the humans wouldn't understand."*

"You heard the other two humans talk," Treacle argued. *"They also know Murray didn't do it."*

"I saw the Unfamiliar attached to Old Murray. I saw it myself, with my witch eyes! What can we do?"

Treacle climbed the wire fence and walked at the top, balancing with his tail. *"What did the dog see? We never found out if it was the same sight. I'm curious."*

I tried to explain through my panic. *"There's a human saying about what curiosity always does to cats!"*

It was too late. Treacle had caught sight of Burger, alone in the kennel, lying down. Treacle gave a loud *miaow*. Burger perked an ear up but otherwise didn't move. Treacle jumped down and swaggered over to the giant, shaggy dog.

Burger whimpered, got up, and sent the thought, *"What do you want?"*

Treacle stretched and yawned. He approached Burger. *"I chased a mouse today. I caught it, then I let it go, then I caught it again. It was fun."*

Burger waited for more.

"Maybe it's not as fun for the mouse. But maybe it is. I thought I'd see." With that, Treacle batted Burger on the nose with one paw.

Burger scoffed and lay back down. *"Leave me alone."*

Treacle didn't. *"I don't understand why everybody here is so miserable."*

"My human is gone. We were such a small pack, just the two of us." Burger whimpered again. *"Of course I'm miserable. Cats can't understand. You're all so selfish."*

"We're understanding each other now. How did that happen? You understand cats?" Treacle wondered.

Burger flicked an ear. *"When I was a puppy, our pack was three: the human, and me, and an old Siamese cat. I grew up knowing what a hiss meant."*

"There are plenty of humans everywhere in this part of the mountains," Treacle said. *"They like dogs too. If your human doesn't come back, I'm sure you'll find another."*

"My human isn't coming back. Go away, cat." Burger began to growl.

Treacle didn't move. *"Tell me to go away again, but without the growl."*

"Go away," Burger thought.

"How did you do that?" Treacle asked.

Burger sent a wave of confusion. *"I... we... just do..."*

"Was this so easy with your human?"

"No." Burger whimpered. *"It never needed to be! Why do you keep bothering me about my human?"*

"Because I want to tell you that not all humans have magic."

Burger stood straight up and growled. *"You are dangerous."*

"Me? What about you! You're bigger!" Treacle fluffed up, tensing for a fight.

Burger lunged forward with a great bark. Treacle fled for the fence opposite the dog. My cat scrambled up that fence, almost losing his footing when Burger crashed her body into it. But Treacle landed on the other side.

"I saw your magic human!" Burger barked furiously. *"I saw the magic that was not human! They worked together to kill my human!"*

"Cath wasn't even at the cemetery that night!" Treacle argued. His fluffy fur flattened again, and he licked his paw to wash his face. *"Talk sense, dog."*

Finally, Burger gave his testimony. Samantha had walked Burger around that night. The cemetery was just another part of the park-meadow to her, though she wouldn't let Burger pee on the gravestones. She could be respectful of the dead, but she was never afraid.

That night, Samantha should have been afraid. Burger had sensed a chill in the air, like the sky was being torn up. He bit on his leash and tried to lead Samantha away, but Samantha was strict and stubborn, and she couldn't sense what was coming. He remembered her telling him, "We always walk this way, Burger! Come on, what's wrong with you?"

The graveyard glowed with moonlight. Burger couldn't see as well as a cat could, but Samantha should have seen... if she'd only thought to look... if she could only believe...

A human was floating in the air toward them. The lower half, at least, seemed like a human. The upper half looked as if it were made out of smoke. The smoke spoke. *This is the one. Kill her and raise the dead.*

Burger didn't know what to make of the smoke, but he lunged at the floating leg and got his teeth in. The floating body waved its hand, and a gust of some kind of force threw Burger against a mausoleum, snapping the leash. Samantha fainted, or seemed to.

Then a tombstone shattered, the earth opened up, and the bones of Shelley Marina emerged from them and lurched toward Samantha. The bones grew gristle at every step.

"Ooh…" the syllable came from the half-formed throat of the ghoulish apparition. "Noo… die… let… me… die…"

The bones collapsed beside Samantha Perry's body and struck her before getting up and trying to continue on. Samantha Perry was already dead. Blake had said that the bruises were post-mortem.

"I was afraid of this thing that I never saw before! Humans aren't supposed to fly!" Burger barked. *"I was afraid! So I ran, and I went back later in the morning to find my human was dead! I should have protected her!"*

"Treacle!" Blake called. It seemed that he'd gone out to see what all the noise was about. Blake scooped up Treacle in his arms and carried the cat away.

I thought about what Burger had shown Treacle—us. *"The full moon and the Unfamiliar made Old Murray fly. That explains the lack of footprints. The Unfamiliar…"*

"Was it the same one?" Treacle asked me.

It was indeed the same Unfamiliar that I'd encountered and sent away from Old Murray at the theater. I was certain of it, even more now that I'd seen it through Burger's eyes. Well, through Treacle's mind's eyes looking through

Burger's eyes. *"Just come home to me and Astrid, Treacle. This was a risk."*

Treacle would never admit that he was wrong. *"Burger bit the human part."*

"There was no human part. It's a whole human and a whole Unfamiliar squished together. So what if Burger managed to bite him?" I wondered, without really wondering.

Blake set down a saucer of milk for Treacle, who began to lap it up. Treacle wondered, *"Did Old Murray have a bite on his leg?"*

"What's the latest with Peanut Butter then?"

Aunt Astrid's voice pulled me back to reality. I'd been in a trance while my mind followed Treacle to the animal shelter.

"That was Treacle," I said. "The Unfamiliar that I saw at the theater was the same as the one that Samantha Perry's dog witnessed. If Old Murray has a month-old bite mark on his leg, then we can confirm that Old Murray was haunted by this Unfamiliar spirit."

Aunt Astrid took a bite of a sandwich and nodded thoughtfully. "Treacle is trying to help the case. Be a dear and reheat the soup. I think it's gone tepid again."

"I don't think cats can understand how complicated humans make things!" I set the microwave to heat the soup again. "This is all well and good to know, but none of it would be admissible as evidence in court. We certainly can't tell Blake—Detective Samberg—"

"Or any other investigators," Aunt Astrid added.

"Yeah." Why had I singled out Blake? I pushed the thought aside and continued. "I'll bet Old Murray's Unfamiliar would have healed his leg anyway."

I poured the soup into two bowls. Aunt Astrid carried her bowl of soup and the plate with all of the sandwiches to the table. I carried my bowl of soup and the giant bowl of salad.

We ate for a while, then Aunt Astrid said, "Not necessarily."

It had been long enough that I'd forgotten what she would be talking about. "Not necessarily to what?"

"The Unfamiliar healing the physical injury of their host. Most Unfamiliar spirits never had human bodies and wouldn't know to do that."

I remembered watching an old movie about a little girl who was haunted by what the Greenstones would call an Unfamiliar. In a famous scary scene, it forced her to turn her head so that her face looked behind her, like an owl... not a human. A human body couldn't survive that.

She should have had broken her neck at that moment. But if an Unfamiliar wasn't familiar with a human body, then...

I shuddered in horror. That little girl in the movie could have been me.

"Of course," Aunt Astrid added, "it depends on what the motive is."

I munched on a lettuce leaf. "Now I'm confused. You told me that the Unfamiliars don't understand basic survival. How can we possibly understand what their motives are then?"

"Motive is a mental thing. Many other motives are much more in the realm of the other world than in the realm of the body. Remember Queen Myrtha?"

She was talking about the ballet, the queen of the ghosts. All of the ghosts were women who'd killed themselves out of unrequited love, or because they'd married somebody who'd cheated on them, or something.

"Imagine Queen Myrtha as Unfamiliar," Aunt Astrid continued. "She wants something from our world, and she's crossing lines and boundaries to take it. Nobody can know why. *But* the only method she knows to get whatever she wants depends on tempting all those other poor girls with the promise of getting what they want."

"Vengeance. The Wilis were the ghosts of women scorned." I remembered reading something like that on the ballet program. "When Giselle forgave those two jerks, Queen Myrtha didn't have any power anymore."

"Exactly." Aunt Astrid murmured into her soup, "If only it could be that simple."

"It can be simpler," I said. "Tell Queen Myrtha to get back in line. That's what witches do. That's what we did. Simple! Done!"

"Your mother would be proud of you." Aunt Astrid beamed. She added, "So I hope that you don't take personally that she would also be suspicious that this was so easy."

I took a piece of bread and used it to sop up the bottom of my soup bowl. "Aunt Astrid... whose motives was my Unfamiliar using? Mine?"

Aunt Astrid hesitated. "If you're not sure— and you were the only one of us who was actually there, who was actually being bothered by the Unfamiliar—we may never know."

My mother would be suspicious of getting rid of an Unfamiliar so easily because she gave her life for it. I steeled myself against that thought. We could know. There was a way.

I needed to know.

"It's full moon tonight," I said. "What about we finally try that séance?"

15. The Walking Dead

That afternoon, the moon was a perfectly round smudge of chalky paleness in a dusky blue sky. Aunt Astrid and I sat on my black picnic blanket in front of my parents' graves.

"I know, I know," I said to the gravestones. "I'm early." I turned to Aunt Astrid. "This suddenly got awkward."

"What do you mean?"

"I mean..." I tried to form the words. "Every year, for fifteen years, I've come here to talk to them. I took for granted that they were listening. Now... I don't know. I'm going to talk to them, and I know they're going to hear me, and if I'm lucky, they're going to talk back. That changes things."

Aunt Astrid phrased it better. "Your attitude toward death before was more normal and comfortable for you."

The other world, the one where all the magic was, also seemed to be the afterlife. It was difficult to explore, and witches could only guess what it was like. The séance itself might not work because it was too soon, like with Samantha Perry. It might not work because it was too late, like with Shelley Marina. Just because somebody was dead didn't mean that they weren't not busy. At least, that was the explanation I'd received when I was thirteen and tried to conduct a séance. It might have been more because my magic talent wasn't that strong yet, or at least not strong enough in the direction of necromancy.

Death, even to witches, remained a mystery. Grieving remained a process.

"We can just sit here then," Aunt Astrid said. "It's a lovely afternoon in a lovely graveyard."

So we sat and waited. Eventually, I wondered aloud, "I wonder how Bea's talk with Jake went."

Aunt Astrid waved dismissively. "I'm sure she'll tell us."

"Eventually. Later. I'm wondering how Bea's doing now."

I nudged Peanut Butter with my mind. His anxieties covered me like a wave. Jake's hand waved toward Peanut Butter's face, making Peanut Butter jump back from where he sat on the table. It wasn't a table I recognized from Bea's place.

Jake demanded, "How do we know we're not under surveillance right now?"

Bea cried, "Cath doesn't do that!"

"You know with your magic?"

"That's not possible! Even if it were, I'd trust them!"

"Well, it's impossible for me. I can't live like that…"

There was a shout from outside the room— not any room in Jake's house, I realized. They were at the police station.

"What was that?" Bea stood and went over to the door.

I pulled my mind back to the graveyard, where I sat beside Aunt Astrid. "Oh, no. They're fighting."

Aunt Astrid sighed. "Better than not speaking to each other."

We sat for a little longer.

I said, "They were fighting about whether I would spy on them through Peanut Butter."

"You'd never!" Aunt Astrid said as if on reflex. Immediately, more humbly, she corrected, "You just did. But you'd never after this."

Suddenly, I stood. Aunt Astrid took my cue and stood with me. She moved off the picnic blanket, stepping smartly.

"I want to go home," I said as I bent over and folded up the blanket. "Wait for Bea there with all her favorite chocolates."

"And a divorce lawyer," Aunt Astrid added. She glanced behind her, startled, and said, "Can I help—"

I glanced up, afraid of how much the bystander had heard. Someone was approaching us slowly, step by lurching step. By the dress, I figured that it was a woman. The dress was faded and stained with dirt, but I'd seen it before. I didn't recognize her face, but it wasn't one I would forget if I'd ever seen it in town.

The skin was taut as a drum over her bones. Her eyes were closed, and I wondered if she was some wandering homeless lady, starved and maybe blind... we never see them for too long in Wonder Falls. There was even a search party for Topher, who didn't have a family anymore.

She reeked something awful. I clapped a hand over my nose and mouth in reflex. She smelled awful, yet familiar.

"Cath," Aunt Astrid warned, pulling at my arm. She wrinkled her nose and coughed a little too.

I recognized the smell then. It was the same smell around the body of Shelley Marina. This woman was walking and dead.

"Let's run!" I said.

16. Another Resurrection

Peanut Butter caught me up later on what had happened at the police station. Somebody was screaming. Bea left the room to see where the screaming was coming from, and Peanut Butter followed her. It wasn't exactly logical. Peanut Butter was afraid of everything but would rather stay by his mommy and daddy and be less afraid. Even though his mommy and daddy were going toward the strange new danger.

Together, Bea and Jake rushed through the aisles between the police officers' desks.

They met Police Chief Talbot, who shouted over his shoulder at Diane, "Put that down and stop dialing! I said that we have a direct line!"

"Direct line to what?" Jake asked. "Who was shouting?"

"Our prime suspect in the Perry case, of course," Talbot answered. "Murray Willis. Looks like a heart attack in the interrogation—hey!"

Bea ran toward the interrogation room despite Chief Talbot's objection. She ran past Diane, who spoke into the phone that had a direct line to the hospital, "Hi, this is Officer Diane Davis, requesting an ambulance at the Wonder Falls police department. Please hurry!"

"Where's your wife going?" Talbot asked Jake.

"I'll get her," Jake said to the police chief.

When he caught up to Bea, she had her face and hands pressed to the glass window of the interrogation room. "That's not a heart attack. It's something else. I can see it! I need to get in there—I need to help him!"

Jake didn't hesitate. He rapped his knuckles against the door until Jason, one of the other officers, unlocked it for him.

Jason swung open the door but said, "Jake, we can't have random civilians passing by and— even if she is your wife—"

"She knows how to resuscitate him," Jake said as Bea bolted in.

Jason frowned as she passed. "So do I, and that's what I was doing. But did you"—he turned to Jake—"stop me just now so that she could…" He turned back to Bea, who was on her knees beside Old Murray. Her eyes were closed and she was waving a hand over Old Murray's unconscious body. "Do nothing? She's not doing CPR. That is not CPR."

"I'll take it from here then," Jake assured him then locked him out. Jake knelt at Old Murray's other side. "What does it look like?"

"A heart attack," Bea said decisively. "But only because that's where the knot is."

"The knot?"

"Where Cath put the Unfamiliar. A binding spell. She can't get rid of the thing, only tie it up so it won't do any more damage to the host. The knot is still there, but the Unfamiliar is gone."

Back at the graveyard, Aunt Astrid and I outran the smell. It wasn't difficult to outrun a corpse, which walked so slowly.

"How do we kill it?" I asked.

Aunt Astrid raised an eyebrow. "Ruthless! She hasn't done anything to us, other than come near when she smells bad."

"She's supposed to be dead," I argued. "If this body is anything like Shelley Marina, killing her would be a mercy. But this is impossible!"

"Saying that this is impossible obviously won't stop it from happening," Aunt Astrid said.

"I know her," I said, "but I don't want to wait until she grows back completely. Where's her gravestone? Can we walk around to take a look?"

We could, and we did, jogging over the turf in the afternoon sunlight. The corpse turned slowly when it heard us and inched toward the grave she'd left. On the gravestone, it said—

"Dolores Thompson. 1946 to 2009. Thompson! I thought I knew that dress." I turned to Aunt Astrid. "It belonged to Tommy's grandmother!"

"She was buried in it." Aunt Astrid nodded. "I wasn't at the funeral, but I heard when she passed away. Breast cancer."

"She was only sixty-three," I said gloomily. I hadn't been at Tommy's grandmother's funeral either.

A death rattle sounded behind us, like, "Taaa...mmm..."

"I think," I said, as I covered my nose and mouth with my sleeve, "she's calling for Tommy. How do we tell her?"

Aunt Astrid stepped between myself and Dolores and declared, "You can join him in the grave!"

"But how?" I wondered. "The bones are moving with some magic force, must be, because the muscles haven't even all grown back. That magic is borrowed by an Unfamiliar, but the only one I've seen in this town recently is bound to Old Murray. I tied it all up myself. Shelley Marina grew back her gristle because Samantha Perry died. Whose life force is Dolores taking to even walk toward us?"

17. Bloodline

"That made no sense to me," Jake said to Bea.

"It doesn't have to," Bea said distractedly. "I'm just thinking aloud. Look, there's a magic knot in his chest. It's slowly draining him of energy, maybe even his life. I'm going to untie it, and if the Unfamiliar is in there anyway... Jake, you run. Do you understand?"

"No," Jake answered. Then he said tensely, "I'm not going to leave you if this unleashes some demon from another dimension either."

Peanut Butter wandered in and *miaowed* plaintively. He'd been diligent with Marshmallow's magic lessons. He saw Bea's hand in the other world, struggling against the knot and forcing it to loosen.

"Almost there," Bea breathed.

Jake didn't see anything, but he kept quiet.

"They can't break," Bea realized. "The bond between Old Murray and... they share a bloodline." She opened her eyes then opened her otherworldly eyes with a new clarity.

At that moment, Dolores Thompson collapsed into a heap of bones in front of Aunt Astrid and myself.

"What just happened?" I said.

Astrid peered at the air around Dolores's unmoving corpse. "Not a single Unfamiliar to be seen."

"Blake is going to lose sleep over this," I muttered. "We've got to get her back into her coffin before anybody sees."

"Catch me," Bea said to Jake, back at the police station. "I'm going to faint."

"Why are you going to faint?" Jake asked.

She answered as she put both of her hands over Old Murray's chest. "The drain on Old Murray's life isn't happening anymore, but it did happen."

Peanut Butter put his paws over Bea's hands and miaowed anxiously.

Jake tried again to make sense of Bea's rambles about magic. "He needs his life restored… and it's coming from you?" His expression quickly changed from confusion to apprehension.

"It won't kill me," Bea assured him and Peanut Butter. "But it's taking a lot out of—"

Then she fainted. Jake caught her.

By the time afternoon had turned into evening, Aunt Astrid and I were patting flat the pieces of turf atop Dolores Thompson's grave. I'd had to break into the groundskeeper's tool shed to steal two shovels.

"More than one Unfamiliar in town," I offered. "At least one witch without training. Another secret society, with a book of magic, who sin against nature."

"Wrath of ancient gods," Aunt Astrid added. "Curses that the dead shall walk the earth, outnumber the living, and eat our brains."

"Maybe we can try to ask the Maid of the Mist if this is just something that happens once a month in Wonder Falls for maybe so-and-so number of months every three hundred years or something."

"It would have been in the Greenstone family record."

Aunt Astrid and I went back to the tool shed to return the shovels.

"I think I know how Blake feels now," I remarked. "If he were only in the know, I could leave him voice messages in the wee hours of the morning, containing the increasingly improbable theories of witches."

"Let's start with what we do know then," Aunt Astrid said. "Try to keep it as simple as possible." Aunt Astrid's phone rang. She took it out of her pocket, and I dusted off my hands as she reacted to the call. "Hello? What happened? Oh, dear."

When she hung up, I said, "The simplest explanation would be that I'm just not very good at binding Unfamiliars."

"We'll ask Bea about that," Aunt Astrid said to me. "That was Jake. He says that she undid your binding on Old Murray. They're both in the hospital."

Jake hadn't told us how bad it was, so Aunt Astrid and I rushed to the hospital, expecting the worst. We found him and Bea in the hospital lobby. Bea leaned against Jake's shoulder, looking exhausted. He was laughing about something as

Aunt Astrid and I approached, and eventually Bea gave a tired chuckle as well.

I said to them, "I'm glad to see that you both patched things up."

"Bea was telling me about burnout," Jake explained. He must have meant magic burnout, which happened when a witch used too much magic.

"And you're all right with that?" I asked, still sounding suspicious.

"It's not that different from keeping her comfortable during that time of the month," Jake said.

Then it was Aunt Astrid's turn to look suspicious. "And you're all right with that?"

Jake and Bea laughed together, in their own world.

Aunt Astrid and I looked at each other, and I knew that we were both thinking the same thing. It couldn't have been this easy. We looked at Jake until he remembered that we had arrived and that we both were waiting for more of an explanation.

Bea said, "Old Murray's in aftercare for cardiac arrest. I came in with low blood pressure."

Aunt Astrid sat beside Jake and asked, "And what's the real story?"

I sat beside Bea, and they caught us up on what happened.

Jake finished with, "I've been a coward. These are things I thought I couldn't understand even if you explained them to me. All I've known since the visit to the animal shelter was that this was dangerous. Bea showed me today that magic also heals."

I gave Jake an exasperated expression. "That was obvious."

"All right," Jake said, "I'm sorry that it took the danger of losing Bea today to get me to wake up to the fact that I don't want to spend any more time apart than we have to."

I thought, sarcastically, that we were so lucky to have life-threatening situations come up like this to save marriages... that shouldn't have been so rocky in the first place, if anybody was willing to communicate.

To test Jake, I said, "You won't have a problem then with the fact that the Greenstones never stay dead, but as witches, we rise from the graves to sustain our eternal youth by drinking blood."

Jake didn't miss a beat. "Nobody's perfect. Considering that blood is the private property of their owners until donated, however, I would be duty-bound to arrest your ancestors if not all transactions are conducted above board."

Bea chuckled.

"What?" Jake said. "I was serious. Was Cath joking? I thought she was explaining more about the Greenstone legacy—"

Bea hushed her husband with a kiss. Aunt Astrid gave them a satisfied smile.

"Anyway," I continued, "at this point, even if we Greenstones explained everything that we knew to each other about the past month, we wouldn't understand it."

Aunt Astrid and I told them about what had happened at the graveyard earlier that afternoon.

When we'd finished, Bea said, "It does make sense now. Dolores Thompson was the one taking Murray Willis's life force."

"No, wait," I said, "Burger witnessed Samantha Perry's death, which was instant. The Unfamiliar was making Old Murray fly around at that time too. It was there, and it was powerful."

Aunt Astrid finished, "Dolores Thompson's life force was slow because of Murray's age. We saw no Unfamiliars at the graveyard. Did you see one at the police station, Bea? Even when you loosed the binding?"

Bea shook her head.

Jake cleared his throat then made an effort to ask, casually, "So you managed to get Burger's, umm... testimony?"

I nodded. "Burger gave Old Murray a nasty bite."

Bea blurted, "No, he didn't."

The three of us looked at her.

"I heal people, remember?" Bea said. "I have an intuition for injury. I would have noticed a month-old bite mark while I was healing Old Murray."

I asked, "Even if the Unfamiliar had healed him?"

"I would have noticed traces of Unfamiliar interference too," Bea said with certainty.

Jake said, "And you mentioned something about bloodline?"

"Hey," I realized, "Old Murray and Dolores Thompson are related, right?"

At that, Aunt Astrid said, "It would explain the connection between them. Not so much with Samantha Perry and Shelley Marina."

"That's why!" I realized. "For all the Unfamiliar's power, the night that Samantha Perry died... if Shelley Marina wasn't drawing life force from the same genetic pool, then the resurrection would fizzle out on its own. If they did share a bloodline, however…"

"You're saying," Jake said, leaning forward, "that Dolores Thompson could have come back to full life and health."

"And Old Murray would have died," Bea said.

Aunt Astrid said, "But then the Unfamiliar wouldn't have a host. They usually latch on to just one person. Crossing from their world into ours is difficult for them."

"Unless," I said, "some people already have a close enough bond for the Unfamiliar to move between. The Unfamiliar could have moved straight to Dolores Thompson."

Bea scratched her head, thought about it, and sighed. "I just don't feel like Old Murray was involved at all in the magical sense, not until this afternoon."

We sat around in silence for a while, lost in our thoughts.

Then I wondered, "Where's Peanut Butter?"

Jake answered, "I called Blake and Cody Willis over from the animal shelter. They arrived before you, and I left Blake to babysit Peanut Butter."

Bea beamed. "Peanut Butter's our baby."

"You know," Jake said, with a tone of mock suspicion, "he doesn't look anything like me…"

"Oh, don't even joke," I said.

But Bea laughed and snuggled against him again. They'd hardly heard me.

I put my face in my hands and released a groan of aggravation. "I don't know what to do with everything that's been happening."

Aunt Astrid reached over Jake and Bea to give me a comforting pat on the knee. "We won't have our next clue until next month."

I groaned again, even though I knew that Aunt Astrid meant that to be comforting.

"I'm hungry," Bea said.

Jake stood. "I'll get Peanut Butter, then we can head home for dinner." He turned to Aunt Astrid and me. "Both of you are welcome to join us, of course."

Aunt Astrid nodded. "I'd love to."

"I'll pass," I told him. I waved good-bye and walked away.

18. Night Jog

For dinner, I ordered a five-cheese pizza. It was still early in the evening when it came, only slightly later when I'd finished half of it, and properly nighttime by the time I felt I'd digested it. Since I felt guilty about binging like that, I decided to go for a jog around the neighborhood.

Sometimes I resented living in this town. In general, nobody liked to be singled out for gossip, but everybody liked to have a target to gossip about. They would say it was because they cared, and that was easy to believe when almost everybody knew each other. I was always wary about that though. How could anybody really know each other?

On the upside, as I said, nobody liked to be singled out for gossip. That kept most people's behavior in line. The Wonder Falls police department had nothing to do most days. It was usually a crime-free town, but that didn't mean it didn't have mysteries.

It was a chilly night. As my jog went on, I panted out white wreaths of mist. With each step kicking off the pavement, I imagined the momentum taking me one step closer to the solution.

"Cath!" Min's voice called behind me.

I jogged in place then turned around. "Hi, Min. I can't stop. I've got to keep my heart rate up."

He was dressed for jogging too. "I'll race you to the falls," he said as he jogged alongside me.

"Through the woods? I didn't bring my flashlight though." As we turned beyond the glow of the streetlamps though, I saw that Min's sneakers had lights at the toes. "So," I panted, as we jogged over the meadow, "did you find Topher?"

"Nuh-uh," Min replied. He had joined the search party that morning. "I'm still getting to know this town again, so I'm not that much help."

"Wish I could have joined," I said, "but, you know, family comes first. We didn't even catch up on rebuilding the Brew-Ha-Ha today."

"Is Blake part of the family again?"

I did a double take. "What, who? Him? Why would Blake be part of the family?"

"Bea's husband," Min corrected himself. "Jake. Blake. Blah, names."

I laughed. "It is kind of cute that they're partners and they rhyme. It sounds like a TV show, but to answer your question, apparently yes—Jake is part of the family again."

If Bea felt as though everything was all right in her marriage again, then I would support her.

We jogged through the meadow, down the slope, and into the woods.

"It must be good to have a family," Min remarked.

"Must be?" I gave him a playful shove. "Min, you have a family!"

"Don't I know it," Min exclaimed flatly. "I just feel bad for Topher, somewhere out there all alone."

Bea was usually the one who had intuitions about people. Min had kept things from me before that almost cost him his life.

I peered at him suspiciously. "It's not just that, is it? What's wrong with your dad?"

"Nothing!" Min told me. He jogged ahead, over the bridge.

I jogged faster to catch up. "Why didn't your dad join us at the show?"

"He never was a social butterfly."

"Was that the reason?" I pressed.

"I'll race you down the riverbank when the moon comes out!"

"If I win the race to the falls, you have to tell me."

Min stopped.

"Oh, come on!" I whined, jogging to turn around.

"I don't know what's going on with my dad," Min confessed. "That's why I need to find Topher."

"What, to distract yourself from your own problems?" I couldn't believe it. "Is that where your newfound sense of philanthropy is coming from after all?"

Min looked hurt. "Cath, it's nothing like that! You couldn't be further from the truth."

"Enlighten me then!"

During the day, the river waters were clear in the sunlight, never muddy, not even after a storm. Now the full moon cast its white light over the same rivers, and the waves and eddies made oily black shapes like ink. I wondered what could be hiding in those waters.

The moment that thought crossed my mind, something surfaced.

"Get back!" I called to Min.

It wasn't something coming out of the water, I realized, but someone. That someone lurched onto the banks.

"It told me you'd be here!" a familiar old man's voice rambled. "It told me to wait, but then it told me to wait, but I'm not waiting another moonshine." He lifted an emaciated hand to point at Min. "You're next…"

The figure stepped into the moonlight. It was Topher.

"Min," I said, "did you bring your cell phone?"

He nodded. "I'll call the cops."

"The hospital," I corrected. "The old man must be freezing!"

As Min made the call, I hauled Topher up on land. One of his trouser legs caught on a nearby reed. As I untangled it, I saw the fading bite mark on his leg. There was no denying it now. If it wasn't Old Murray, then Topher had been the Unfamiliar's host all along.

"What did it tell you?" I demanded.

"You fool!" an ethereal voice hissed somewhere about him. "I told you, not with the witch with him!"

"And the Maid of the Mist so nearby," I added. "Do you think you won't lose if we fight it out right now? I'll call my Familiar, who will call my cousin and my aunt, and they'll bring their Familiars—then you won't stand a chance! We're both at full power at this moon phase. Let's fly around and blast magic fireworks at each other. Even if Min sees it, nobody would believe him." It was a boast. I couldn't fly on full moon nights, not even with a broomstick.

Then the Unfamiliar presence did something unexpected. *Mercy*, it begged.

"You came into my hometown and threatened my people," I said to it. "One of them is dead. Then you attacked me. How dare you even ask! How dare you!"

Mercy for you as well, it said slyly. *I can never win, that is true. But what will you lose so that I lose? Your binding was a mercy.*

"And that didn't work," I told it. "I won't try that again."

Will you do what your mother did? Not even for a child but for the sake of one not long for this world anyway. Give your life, and the life of the one with you, and the life of this body which I hold—all to ensure that I never come back here again. Will you?

"Yes." I stepped back and reached my mind out to the moonlight—

Motives! it shouted desperately. *The other witch said! The other witch thought! At the dance! There is another way. Why would you not take it?*

"Why would you suggest that? Why are you trying to help me?"

It replied, *You are a cat with a mouse. You will play with your prey. You want to find another way. I have a chance if you have a chance.*

"I shouldn't make deals with your kind. They never work the way we think."

Then came a voice like a rainstorm. "I am bound to this cause, that you understand this arrangement completely."

I looked around even though I sensed that the voice didn't come through my ears. I saw the Maid of the Mist flowing toward us from the shaded bridge. In the moonlight, she looked like a sigh of breath in the cold night, wreaths of fog floating in the shape of a woman. She moved like a ghost but with more life and purpose.

"The choice is yours, Cath Greenstone," she said. "Seal this door with the blood of all those the moonlight touches, or risk this Unfamiliar tipping the balance between my world and yours—for a hope that all may live."

"You're the Maid of the Mist," I said resentfully. "You could seal the door without bloodshed. Don't you have that power?"

She shook her head slowly. "We keep the balance. We follow our laws."

This all really was up to me then.

"You have to keep the balance," the Maid of the Mist said to me. "Find a way."

"And if I don't, will you step in?"

"Find a way," she repeated. "This thing has no power until the next full moon. You have to get Topher to release the Unfamiliar until then."

When I blinked, she was gone.

Topher curled up in a ball and trembled. "Why isn't it working? Where's Dolly?"

Min Park approached me. "Cath, we're in the middle of the meadows, so I can't give the paramedics a street address…"

"Tell them to meet us at the corner of Ebb and Eddy," I told him. "Old Mr. Thompson can make it there without a stretcher if he has our help. Isn't that right, Topher?"

Mournfully, Topher said to me, "You've got yourself a deal!"

I knew that he hadn't understood a single word I'd said to him.

"Was someone else here with us?" Min asked as Topher laid an arm over one of my shoulders. Min himself got under Topher's other arm. "I thought I saw someone, but then I didn't. She looked familiar..."

Topher answered happily, "Oh, yes, my Alice is a beauty. Come to help your old man, Tommy?"

"Yeah," I said, "there are a lot of people with us, here in Topher's head."

The Unfamiliar gave a sinister chuckle.

19. A Dungeon for the Insane

Topher's body had sustained no permanent injuries from wandering around. He lacked sleep and, ironically, hydration. He had no frostbite. He was obviously demented, so by morning, the attending doctors agreed to move him to a padded room below the ground level of the hospital.

Min and I went to visit him.

"Like a dungeon," Min said gloomily. "A dungeon for the insane."

At least it was clean, and the orderlies didn't look completely soulless, but I didn't like it either—and not only because I predicted that I'd be spending some days there, interrogating Topher and the Unfamiliar.

The floor had fluorescent lights everywhere. I think that was the worst part of rooms without natural light. I wondered if Wonder Falls had hidden away many other mentally ill people there.

"Don't we have an old folks' home in this town?" Min wondered.

"We do. I don't think they can help him as much there."

Min tried to stifle a yawn.

"I'm getting you home," I said. It had been a long night. "Where is home for you, by the way?"

"With my parents," he grumbled.

Min had the money to buy a house anywhere in Wonder Falls. A mansion, even, one designed to his tastes and built with the best materials. He'd stayed at a hotel when he first came back— and from that hotel room, he'd been kidnapped, terrorized, and almost killed. Since then, Mrs. Park wouldn't let him sleep anywhere that wasn't under her watchful eye.

At that moment, Min's cell phone beeped. He read the text message with bleary eyes. "It's my dad. I told him we found Topher and that I was waiting at the hospital... he's upstairs, ready to take me home."

"That's a bit much," I exclaimed.

Mr. Park had been cold and distant while Min was growing up, and that actually wasn't all that bad because Mr. Park was cold and distant to everybody. To come by for the sole purpose of hauling Min away was unlike him. Then again, if I'd learned anything from what had happened between Bea and Jake, it was that I should stay out of other people's relationships.

We had a long pause until he said, "I'll tell him not to and be right back."

"Take your time." In hindsight, I realized that Min had been waiting for me to offer to go upstairs with him. But I didn't offer, and maybe he'd thought it would be too emasculating or something if he asked.

Eventually, a nurse rolled in a wheelchair with Topher in it.

He looked directly at me. "You witch."

"Yes," I said, "this witch. It's going to be just you and me now." To the nurse, I asked, "What's his room number?"

"B2-9." She gave me a look when I walked alongside the wheelchair. She must have expected me to stay outside the room. "Are you family?"

"I brought him here," I explained. "My friend called the ambulance. He doesn't really have a family."

Topher shook his head. "Dolly. She's back."

The nurse frowned. "He's really not lucid."

"That's why we're rolling him in here, isn't it?" I sounded too callous. That wouldn't get anything done.

Topher insisted, "Dolly's back!"

I explained to the nurse, "Dolores Thompson was his wife's name. Dolly for short, you see?" I was guessing, but I guessed pretty well. "She passed away years ago." I continued, affecting a casual carelessness, "I think she was also the sister of Topher's best friend—Murray Willis. He's in the heart ward of this very same hospital, in recovery. I heard he was put in here just yesterday afternoon."

The nurse relaxed. Topher, on the other hand, whimpered protests against what he now knew that I knew.

"So you're the closest thing he has to family right now," the nurse said as we stopped at the door.

I shook my head modestly. "I'm just doing what I can to help." To Topher, I said, "I'll visit as often as I can." To the nurse, I asked, "Are there visiting hours?"

She pushed the wheelchair into the room, and I helped her lift Topher out of the wheelchair and onto a padded gurney. "There must be, but nobody ever visits, so we've all forgotten. You won't be allowed in the room after this." The door shut behind us with a muffled thump. The nurse rolled back the wheelchair and gestured toward the door. "You see, no door handle on the inside. It can only be opened from the outside." She pushed a panel in the padded wall beside the door, and it sprung open to reveal a single push-button, which she pushed. "We're really understaffed, so we can't have anyone just waiting on you for as long as you would visit."

An orderly came by to open the door.

Topher cried more loudly.

To the nurse, I said, "Could I just stay a little longer? I'll calm him down and say good-bye."

The nurse nodded to the orderly and said, "She's all right. We'll come back in ten." Then they both left.

"I'm sorry for everything that's happened to you in your whole life," I said to Topher. "I'm also sorry for what's going to happen, which will actually be my fault."

I needed to get Topher to talk. I hated what I was about to do, even more that I told myself that I had to do it. I hated that I got into situations where I had to be so awful.

20. Mr. Park

I belted his wrists with the straps on either side of the bed. His expression seemed apprehensive, but he didn't have the presence of mind to resist me.

I barred my arm against the defenseless old man's throat and told him, "You don't have a family. If I crushed your neck right now so that you couldn't breathe, nobody would miss you."

Topher's old eyes met mine fearfully.

"I'd do it if it would stop you from killing people! Why Samantha? Why Old Murray? What are you trying to do? Tell me!"

"Tommy," he said tremulously. "Not Alice. Can't with Alice. Bring them back."

"How?" I demanded. "What did it promise you?"

"It showed me that it could!" he wailed. "It showed me how! Your man…"

My man? I backed away. "Do you mean Min? Min Park? He's a friend."

He shook his head.

"Why him?" I asked. "Why any of these people?"

He continued to shake his head.

I put my hand against his throat and shouted, "Answer me! Why are you so fixated on Min Park?"

The door slammed open. Mr. Park stood in the doorway, and he looked at me with an expression that I'd never seen on his face. He was afraid. But he told me in a stern and commanding voice, "Leave him alone. Step back."

He wasn't afraid of me. He wasn't even afraid for me.

I stepped back as Min jogged up behind his father.

"Cath," Min said, "what are you doing?"

"She was going to kill this poor old man!" Mr. Park declared.

"That's a lie!" More of a mistake really. Unfortunately, it was an easy mistake to make. It was true, though, that I wasn't going to kill

Topher—not on purpose. I was only threatening him. I knew that wouldn't have sounded better.

Mr. Park demanded, "What are you doing in this room then?"

I shot back, "What are you doing opening the door to this room? You're not an orderly. That's not allowed."

"Tell the orderly! I will tell them what I saw."

The nurse strode up to us and hissed, "What's going on? You're being very noisy and upsetting the patients."

Mr. Park and I glared at each other. Then Mr. Park told the nurse what he'd seen me doing. I didn't know how to win that argument, and I didn't feel like I could. With the look on the nurse's face—shock, then betrayal, then contempt—I wouldn't even try.

Min looked from me to his father, not sure what was going on. "This is crazy. I'm leaving."

"You should all leave," the nurse said.

I walked from the hospital to the Brew-Ha-Ha. I staggered, more like, because I was sleepy and miserable. Long walks usually gave me time to think, but with every step, I could only think about how I'd ruined everything. I wondered if the nurse would file a police complaint.

Bea and Aunt Astrid were already there. They could tell instantly that something had gone horribly wrong, and they ushered me into the cellar of the Brew-Ha-Ha. I flopped onto two of the three beanbag chairs and begged them to leave me alone. So they did. Aunt Astrid shut off the lights.

My eyes burned with sleepiness, but my worries wouldn't let me drift off to a peaceful rest. I was heartbroken by the possibility that the awful things I'd said and done to Topher would all have been for nothing.

When I did sleep, I didn't dream.

I woke to Bea flicking on the lights. I was lying on the tatami mat—I must have rolled off the beanbags while I was asleep. Treacle and Peanut Butter bounded down the staircase and rubbed against me while I sat up.

"Dinner!" Aunt Astrid announced as she descended the stairway with two plates. She set one on the table in front of me. "My attempt at Ted's vegan poutine recipe."

The smell made my mouth water and my stomach grumble. "Vegan poutine. This is real witchcraft."

Bea added, "If it turns out all right, we can add it to the menu."

It was all right, I supposed. I was too hungry to really critique the dish in more detail than "edible." On top of everything else, I was crying as I ate, tears that I didn't bother to wipe away, and I tried to chew and swallow between sobs.

Once I was done being a mess, I confessed to Aunt Astrid and Bea what had happened that left me such a mess: the evening jog with Min Park, finding out who the real host of the Unfamiliar was, the deal I'd made with the Maid of the Mist, and finally how I turned Topher into a ticking time bomb of otherworldly horror... and ensured that we could never again get near enough to defuse him.

I was sorry. I was so, so sorry.

Bea and Aunt Astrid moved to either side of me and gave me a hug.

Bea said, "I'm so sorry that you had to go through all that on your own!"

"You did your best," Aunt Astrid added. "And you did give us a month."

I sniffled. "Did Min Park come to help with the renovations?"

They told me that he hadn't. I guessed he was still mad.

21. Woodworking Artist

A waning gibbous moon shone over Wonder Falls.

Aunt Astrid booked an appointment at the Wonder Falls spa for all three of us, because, as she said, we'd have a long month ahead of us. Getting pampered was part of preparing for it. I had my objections, but Aunt Astrid silenced them with, "You're not allowed to run yourself into the ground like you did yesterday."

Bea was reluctant to go to the spa, but she brought Jake, who had no reluctance at all and was very enthusiastic about sauna massages. Chief Talbot had given Jake the day off so that Bea would quit coming to the station and fighting with Jake (or worse—so Talbot said—making up with Jake) in Talbot's office. To Talbot, Bea seemed to have interrupted a crisis in the police department, yet did not help, before promptly becoming dead weight herself... that also counted against her.

I remembered that Jake remarked, "Blake should be here. Talbot forced him to take a vacation too, but Blake's not taking it. He's still investigating."

We came out of the spa a little more relaxed. I particularly liked the massage, almost as much as Jake, and would definitely go back. The relaxation period didn't last long however.

The next day, we spent the afternoon in the cellar of the Brew-Ha-Ha, formulating plans. Bea would research Christopher Thompson's family records, because if Dolores Thompson's relation to Murray Willis was important, then maybe we could predict the next link. Jake would keep us informed of the goings-on in the Wonder Falls police department and their investigation. Aunt Astrid would rally all of our Familiars, which meant a lot of meditating with our cats. If the Unfamiliar had its way by the end of the month, she said, then we would have help.

I would build the digital database for all of Aunt Astrid's dream diaries. The reason for that was obvious to me, even though Aunt Astrid and Bea would never say it—I'd done enough damage.

A waning half-moon shone over Wonder Falls.

The Wonder Falls police department had insufficient evidence to build any sort of case against Old Murray.

Bea visited Old Murray in the hospital and confirmed that Dolores Thompson used to be Dolores Willis—Old Murray's sister. She listened with genuine interest to Old Murray's stories of when he and Topher were young, but he seemed to grow suspicious when Bea asked about the names of their great-grandparents.

Old Murray recovered enough to return to the animal shelter.

Bea then had the bright idea to contact Naomi LaChance. Under the pretense of writing a biography for Thomas Thompson, Bea tried to glean what Naomi knew. Naomi, we knew, was a good friend of Tommy's.

From those conversations, Bea learned that Tommy had been raised by his grandparents, Dolores Willis-Thompson and Topher Thompson. Tommy had never spoken to Naomi about his mother. Naomi confessed to taking Tommy's death as personally as she had for one very simple reason—she and Tommy had been secret high school sweethearts. Not even Bea had known.

In short, Bea found out nothing useful, although that nothingness did have edges, and the empty shape formed by those edges, once filled, could be useful.

A wide waning crescent moon shone over Wonder Falls.

Jake and Blake teamed up once more. Jake told me afterward he'd had to contrive a reason to search Topher's residence so that he wouldn't be tempted to talk to Blake about magic. Jake used the excuse of helping his wife research the biography on Tommy, saying that Tommy's childhood home—Topher's house—would be a good start.

"That's a terrible use of our time as law enforcers," Blake had said, probably with the tactless bluntness he always had.

Jake had ignored him.

In Topher's cabin in the woods, Jake found the living room furniture all piled against the walls as if they'd been caught in a hurricane. The middle of the living room was clear of furniture, and the floorboards had burn marks of perfect circles and sinister-looking glyphs.

Blake walked around, examining the scene. He told Jake that the burn marks on the floor gave him the creeps because they reminded him of the Order, a group of magicians that had targeted Blake. Blake thought the Order were crazy to believe in magic, and thankfully he still thought that, but he'd seen the way that those without magic talents tried to use the forces of the other world anyway. Geometry like that was one way.

Jake tried to move one of the tables that had been shoved against the wall. It had met the wall with enough force to splinter two of the legs, but it was solid teakwood. Jake had to strain to move it an inch, and Topher was old.

Blake became bored and impatient very quickly. He complained that they should continue to look for a murderer in town, the one who had killed Samantha Perry. Jake couldn't tell him that they'd found the killer. So they both left.

After Jake told us Greenstones what he'd found, we went to the Thompson residence to erase the burns on the floor. Looking at them gave me a headache. The symbols galvanized the air with meaning: *Take a life this night.*

I had no doubt that Topher had been in that very room, letting the power of the Unfamiliar burn the wood, and the magic had moved the life force of Old Murray into his dearly departed Dolly.

"This way would have saved him from more dog bites," I remarked, over the sound of the sanding belt that Bea pressed down upon the panels.

Aunt Astrid nodded. "It could be learning. That is a dangerous Unfamiliar. Our advantage is usually that they don't know entirely know how our world works."

I sighed. "This thing needs to be stopped. We better be ready."

I didn't add that we didn't know yet how to stop it.

22. Trumpson

A slim waning crescent moon shone over Wonder Falls.

Bea and I went to do some grocery shopping at the Park family's supermarket. We were pulling out the shopping carts when Mrs. Park approached us.

I was happy to see her, and I said as much before asking, "Is Min here?" More apprehensively, I asked. "Is Mr. Park here?"

"No," Mrs. Park answered. "You shouldn't be here either. Please leave."

Bea sounded shocked. "Mrs. Park! What have we done?"

"Not you," she said to Bea.

"Oh, thanks!" I said, sarcastically. "That's really nice, with all that's happening."

Mrs. Park gave me a look of misery. "Who have you told what Topher told you?"

"He didn't tell me anything!" I whined. Then I straightened up. "Mrs. Park, what do you think he told me?"

The same fearful look that Mr. Park had had at the asylum showed on Mrs. Park's face then.

"If it worries you this much, you can trust me!" I said.

"What if I don't?" Mrs. Park challenged. "Will you handcuff me to the balcony railings and choke me almost to death?"

I flinched. "I've learned that... that's not going to help."

Mrs. Park set her jaw. "You're not the kind little girl that I baked cookies for anymore, who didn't need to be told not to shout and hit people. And this is not your concern."

I objected, "This is my concern, especially if my family is banned from shopping at your store."

"Get out, or I will call the police!"

"Mrs. Park, I don't know what you're so insecure about, but please do not talk to my cousin like that!" Bea grabbed my arm and led me away. "Come on, we'll shop at the farmer's market with Mom. Vegan, gluten-free, organic everything."

"Nooo!" I lunged away from her and collapsed in front of Mrs. Park, grasping at the hem of her apron. "Don't let her take me to that place, Mrs. Park!"

Bea pouted. "It's not that bad! Jake loves the meatloaf I make from the farmer's vegan ground beef!"

Both Mrs. Park and I gave Bea a look of confusion.

"From vegan cows," Bea explained. "The cows are vegan. It's a joke Mom and I... look, never mind! What's all this even about?"

"You really don't know?" Mrs. Park said to Bea, then she looked at me and her expression softened—more than softened but melted, or seemed to because she began to cry. She let out a sniffling sob, pulled her apron hem out of my clutches, and tottered away.

Bea sighed. "That could have gone better. Are you all right, Cath?"

I stood slowly, gathering my thoughts. "Topher's Alice." I turned to Bea. "Topher kept picking on Min for what he 'did to my Alice,' but of course we didn't know any Alice Thompson in school."

Bea shook her head. "Topher's demented."

"No, demented means that you forget. What if he's remembering too much instead? We know that Dolly's real and Tommy's real. We should look for Alice."

The moon did not shine over Wonder Falls. It had blanketed itself completely in the earth's shadow.

As driven as Blake Samberg could be about an unsolved case, he could be easily distracted by petty crimes. Everyone at the Wonder Falls police department understood when Jake, who was supposed to be Blake's partner, threw his hands up in surrender and walked away—just to leave Blake to it. Jake used that time to search the Wonder Falls census. Bea spent her days at the library, searching the obituaries of the Wonder Falls newspaper.

I finished making the database of Aunt Astrid's dreams and thought that I would check up on the animals at the shelter.

When I arrived, Blake, Cody, and Old Murray were putting pet carriers into a van out front.

Cody saw me first and called, "Miss Greenstone! Good time to volunteer today!"

He didn't hate me then, for scaring Burger or getting his grandfather arrested. That was a nice change. I waved as I approached them. "How are you holding up, Murray?"

"Cath," Old Murray nodded, "it's been a while. I don't remember what happened at the show. I'm afraid my mind's going."

"You're looking well today," I offered, trying to comfort him. When he didn't look comforted, I added, "I can take care of myself. You've just got to find somebody to take care of you."

Cody piped up, "Hi!"

"Naw," Old Murray said. "You can't live your life for me, Cody. You've got your own to live. The old folks' home ain't so bad—"

Blake scoffed. "The Wonder Falls old folks' home is worse than most prisons." He moved to the front of the van, opened the passenger side door, and whistled. Burger bounded over and hopped into the passenger seat.

"I meant the idea," Old Murray muttered.

"Is that where you're taking all the animals?" I asked. "To the old folks' home? I'm confused."

Blake buckled the seat belt over Burger. The dog nudged Blake's forehead with his nose, making Blake flinch and back away.

"It was the Park boy's idea," Old Murray said. "Pets that nobody wants meet with people that nobody wants."

"Come with us," Cody said to me. "We could use an extra hand."

I spent the drive there talking with the animals. Most of them didn't want to share their lives with humans. They weren't hostile to the idea, because the Willises didn't include any animals that they knew were wilder than Treacle. Still, the animals didn't want human company so much as trustworthy company at all. Even among animals, that sort of company was more difficult to come by. Burger spent all of his life being looked after by a human. He might have needed human company and attention, but he didn't want one—because what if nobody really could replace Samantha?

We arrived at the old folks' home. From the outside, it looked charming, all red brick walls covered in ivy and an arch over the gate with wrought-iron letters that spelled HELL IN. We unloaded the crates, brought them into the courtyard with great care, and waited. Code and Murray went inside.

I turned to Blake. "It's good that you're taking time away from the case to volunteer like this."

He looked at me so suspiciously that I almost laughed.

"I'm just saying!" I said. "Justice is very important, don't get me wrong, but when there's something wrong in the world that doesn't have a perpetrator, then it's too easy to forget about the victims. It's great to help this way, don't you agree?"

"No," he said. "This is the key to the case."

I sighed. "Okay, Blake, I take it all back. This was a bad idea, and you need more sleep."

"Didn't you read the sign on the way in?" Blake pointed toward the entrance.

I shrugged and read it aloud. "'Hell In.' Not a cheerful name for this place."

"Why are you only reading the letters that are still there?"

"Because," I answered slowly, "it's what's there?"

"Read the letters that rusted at the edges and fell off," Blake said. "Look! It's so obvious!"

"Obvious? I didn't study forensics in Boston."

"It says THE SHELLEY MARINA FOUN-DATION," Blake said.

"Shelley Marina…" I gasped. "The name on the gravestone! The other body I found!" As quickly as it peaked, the feeling of epiphany plummeted to apathy. "So?"

"She was a philanthropist, just like Min Park," Blake said. "Some loophole in inheritance laws meant that her daughter, Rosemary, couldn't inherit after she married Basil Trumpson. Their ashes were scattered over the falls. The grave robber must have thought that the family treasure was buried with Shelley. We have a motive. Now I just have to find the means…"

Out the corner of my eye, I saw Min Park emerge from the home.

"Who did you say Rosemary Marina married?" I asked Blake.

"Basil Trumpson."

Then the idea hit me like a lightning bolt. "You mean Thompson. Basil Thompson. I remember that name in my research. Basil and Rosemary Thompson were cremated. They're the missing link!"

"Thompson must've looked like Trumpson in the old record books. They're ancient and falling apart." Blake shrugged. "Either way, I'm a genius."

I hugged him and said, gleeful again with epiphany, "No, you're not! The grave robbery attempt is the worst idea you've ever spoken out loud to me, and I've heard hundreds by now! You should get more sleep!"

"Now my feelings hurt." Blake frowned. "You're wrong. I won't sleep until I prove it."

I pulled away from him and ran toward the gate, calling behind me, "Then tell the Willises I had a family emergency! Say hello to Min for me!"

23. Next in Line

A slim waxing crescent moon shone over Wonder Falls.

In the cellar of the Brew-Ha-Ha, Aunt Astrid, Bea, Jake, and I met to compare notes. I'd bought a large whiteboard and was struggling to open a pack of markers.

"We found Alice," Jake said.

Bea pulled out a photocopy of a newspaper obituary. "Topher and Dolly's daughter. Tommy's mother. Died in childbirth at the age of sixteen."

Jake added, "Of course she was unmarried. The identity of Tommy's father remains a mystery though."

I said, "People around here must've known who she was. I suppose we could've easily asked around."

"Hmm," Astrid said, looking as though she was trying to remember Alice. "I didn't know the Thompsons well then. Maybe I saw her around and I just didn't pay attention. I certainly didn't hear about her death."

"They probably didn't want to announce it," I said. "Kept it hush-hush. She did give birth out of wedlock. To Topher and Dolores, that must've been scandalous."

"We think she'll be the next to rise from her grave," Bea finished.

Aunt Astrid pondered that. "That's Topher's motive, isn't it? He doesn't want to be alone anymore, having outlived his whole family."

"He's not so careful about not outliving his friends," I said sadly, remembering Old Murray. That wasn't fair of me to say though. The Unfamiliar had made Topher desperate. At last, I got the markers out of their package and got one uncapped. "Let's go over what we know." I scribbled a word on the whiteboard, near the top: Resurrection. "That's what this Unfamiliar always does, because that's what Topher wants to do. The cost for a life is a life. Two full moons ago, for Shelley Marina"—I wrote her name under Resurrection then drew a sideways arrow—"the cost was Samantha." I wrote Samantha Perry next to the arrow. Beside that, I drew an equal sign and the word FAILED.

"They had no blood relation," Bea said. "In a town this small, it's unlikely to not have any blood relation. Samantha was a fairly new resident and didn't grow up here at all."

"The sacrifice for a resurrection," Jake offered, "won't be a random unlucky person again."

I nodded. "They'll still be awfully unlucky, but whoever it is will be more carefully chosen. Not only that, but who is resurrected will be carefully chosen." Shelley Marina's only descendant was Rosemary Marina. Below the previous line, I drew a question mark and the names Rosemary Marina Thompson and Basil Thompson. "Rosemary and Basil were cremated and their ashes scattered over the falls. Why didn't we have ash golems wandering around town in the last full moon?"

Bea riffled through Jake's report. "No living relations on the Marina side still reside in Wonder Falls. Rosemary Marina's father was apparently an Italian celebrity who never set foot in the Americas, or so Shelley said. The townsfolk believed her. Rosemary grew up in unstigmatized illegitimacy."

"In this town?" The disbelief in my tone made the question rhetorical. "Now I'm really sorry to have missed the good old days!"

Aunt Astrid suggested, "It might be because the ashes were washed outside of the Wonder Falls boundaries."

Bea explained to Jake, "The Maid of the Mist claimed the land on which this town was built. Anything beyond that boundary that comes in gets checked or interfered with by the Familiars, same as anything from inside the boundary going out. Anything within is the responsibility of witches to police."

"Then why don't the Familiars stop the Unfamiliars before the Unfamiliars do anything?" Jake wondered.

We all had our own answers that we said at almost the same time.

"Familiars and Unfamiliars are only our words for them," I said. "We don't know which one they are until they do something good or bad, and even then we don't know until the next time they decide to do anything."

"Most magic, whether those are magic spells or magic beings, must follow the rules of space and time," Bea said, "or else it couldn't exist and affect itself here. The Unfamiliar transcend those."

"The Familiars are scared of this one," Aunt Astrid said. "I've gone all over. If worse comes to worst, they won't help us. They really feel that they can't."

"All right. So... the rules of this magic spell are that you can't resurrect your parents or ancestors, but only your descendants?" Jake asked.

"That's a good question. We do know that it resurrects siblings." I drew another moon and the name Dolores Willis Thompson, an arrow, Murray Willis, an equal sign, and the word INTERRUPTED.

Aunt Astrid stood and pointed at the names of the resurrected. "Shelley Marina was first; Dolores Thompson was second. Why this order? Was Topher more eager to have his grandmother back in his life than his wife?"

We thought about it.

"No," I decided. "The boundary of Wonder Falls again. The fact that spells have to follow the rules of time if they're going to have an effect on the temporal world... the Unfamiliar started with resurrecting the oldest body that still remained in town. Topher and the Unfamiliar didn't trade Samantha's life for Tommy's, even though Topher must have missed Tommy more than Shelley."

"So," Bea concluded, "after Dolores, the next to rise would be Alice Thompson. She wasn't cremated, and she was the next generation."

Jake asked, "If Alice Thompson is the next to be resurrected, would the victim be Murray Willis again?"

I quickly scribbled a family tree then changed marker colors to highlight the connection between Murray Willis and Alice Thompson.

"That's possible," Aunt Astrid remarked.

"But it's usually not possible because the sacrificial human didn't survive," Bea added. "And therefore ran out of life force to sacrifice."

"We have a new Plan A then," I said. "We protect Old Murray."

RESURRECTED	SACRIFICE	RESULT
Shelley Marina	**Samantha Perry**	= **FAILED** (no blood relation)
mother of		
Rosemary Marina married to Basil Thompson NOT resurrected - both cremated		
mother of		
Dolores Willis Thompson	**Murray Willis**	= **INTERRUPTED** (blood relation - siblings)
mother of		
Alice Thompson	**Murray Willis again??**	

Jake frowned. "What was the old Plan A?"

I sighed. "To convince Topher not to keep using the power of the Unfamiliar."

Unfamiliars confused people. They fed desperations, obfuscated other options, and all the while could only work with what the hosts gave them. Give them nothing—so simple, yet it always proved impossible.

Later that night, after I'd gone home and gone to bed, I stared at the moon through my window from where I was tucked in and trying to sleep.

Renovations at the Brew-Ha-Ha were complete. With Aunt Astrid doing the baking and cooking—and some of the brewing and mixing—we'd still be understaffed. I'd submitted an ad to the Wonder Falls newspaper. Over the next week, hopefully, there would be applicants to vet and interviews to process.

We didn't have time for that. The moon shone through my window to remind me that we were running out of time.

Treacle had curled up on top of the quilt, over my stomach. He stretched a paw out to try to calm me down.

"No. I feel like we're missing something," I told him. The feeling nagged at me. "We Greenstones have generations of records to study about the way magic works. This Unfamiliar works by trial and error. As Aunt Astrid said, it learns. It's learning its limits. What if the decisions we've decided they're most likely to make turn out to not be the decisions they actually do make?"

"Life is full of surprises," Treacle told me.

"Life is full of fatality," I said.

Treacle yawned. *"We can only do what we do."*

And what did any of this have to do with Min Park and his family?

A wide waxing crescent moon shone over Wonder Falls.

24. Lost

For the next couple of days, I went about my daily routine feeling as if I'd left my wallet somewhere or forgotten to turn off the iron in the house. Nothing regarding Samantha's murder, the unnatural exhumation of not just one but two of the local residents of Wonder Falls Cemetery, the close call Old Murray had escaped thanks to Bea, or the weird behavior of the Parks family seemed to fit together.

No matter how hard I tried, I couldn't help but worry it all like an annoying hangnail. It didn't help that while I was waiting at the animal shelter for Min, Blake showed up. He yanked the door open and stopped for a second, looking at me.

"What are you doing here?" he snapped, sounding a lot like the dogs in the back kennel as they demanded their food.

"I'm waiting on Min. And good morning to you, too."

Blake looked at me then at his watch as if to confirm it was morning. The sun was coming up in the east like usual. I wasn't trying to pull a fast one on him.

He nodded and pulled Dixie cup from the side of the water cooler across from the waiting room seat I was sitting in. After filling the cup with water, Blake tossed it back quickly. He looked tired. Another sleepless night for him too, I thought.

"I don't get this." He flopped down in the seat next to me. "I have turned this thing over and over in my mind a million times. Nothing has clicked, fallen into place, revealed itself, or even seemed to give me a nudge in the right direction. I've never had a case go cold and…" He stared into the space in front of him.

As much as I hated to admit it, I knew how he felt. "I've been trying to put the whole thing out of my mind so maybe I could look at it later with a fresh perspective, you know?"

"That's easy for you to do. You work at the coffee shop," he said, not even looking at me.

I let out a loud sigh, reminding myself Blake was no monument to social graces. Someday he was going to really push the wrong button, and

I would not be responsible for my actions. Until then, I focused on the sound of the dogs barking. It was breakfast time. Cody was entering the kennel with their dog food and a watering can of fresh water. All the furry four-legged beasts were happy to see him.

Before Blake arrived to spread his cheer, I'd tried to talk with Burger again for a little more information. He wouldn't say a word, at least not to me. The pack mentality was nearly impossible to crack through, so even if he had told the other dogs something about his human or that night, they weren't talking to me either.

When Cody appeared again, the bag of dog food in his hand was visibly lighter. No sounds but happy crunching came from the kennel. Cody walked into the waiting room with us and set down the bag.

"So what is Min meeting you here for?" he asked in his usually awkward way, shifting from left foot to right then back again, looking at the ground before letting his eyes meet ours.

"Well, he was thinking of making a little investment in your animal shelter," I said.

"Do we need that? I mean, I think Old Murray and I are doing pretty well on our own, right? Would he be working here too, then?"

I saw Cody was a little nervous about a stranger coming in and up-turning the apple cart. He was comfortable with Old Murray. They were close, and I could understand how a kid like him would prefer things not change.

"He just wants to help, you know, if you guys need more room or repairs. He's looking to give assistance."

"Will he be my new boss?"

"Oh, no. Nothing like that. He'd invest some of his money, but you and Old Murray would still manage the place like you have been."

Cody's face visibly relaxed. That made me relax. Until I saw Blake's face twisted in a scowl of deep thought. He aggravated me by just sitting there. I was about to say something rude to him when my phone rang and cut me off. It was Min.

"Hey, Min. Where are you?"

"You won't believe this, but I got lost."

"How do you get lost in Wonder Falls? You've just lived here your whole life." I couldn't help but tease him.

The truth was if you weren't from Wonder Falls, it was quite easy to get lost. Most towns were planned around a grid pattern with the majority of the streets running north, south, east, and west. Wonder Falls was designed like a snake pit with dozens of windy roads that changed name and direction without warning. One-way streets and dead ends could make a tourist feel as if they are trying to maneuver through a maze. Min had grown up here, but he had been gone for years, and a lot had changed since he was a teenager.

"Where are you now? I'll talk you through it."

"No, no. I've found something interesting." Min's voice was excited.

"Yeah? What is it?"

"The Wonder Falls Orphanage."

I swallowed hard and pursed my eyebrows. Blake looked at me as if he thought he saw a clue on my face. I turned my back to him. It was childish, but the truth was my conversation didn't include him.

"Orphanage? Where? Are you sure you're in Wonder Falls?" I asked. "Maybe you stumbled into unincorporated Frankfort. I didn't know there was an orphanage here. Is it even open?"

"Yes, it's open. There are no children here, if that's what you mean. But it's still open. You've got to see this place. It's exactly what I'm looking for."

"Well, give me the address, and I'll be right there."

Blake's head looked in my direction, but I didn't acknowledge him. Instead I stood and headed out the door to my car, giving Cody a wave and smile good-bye.

As I got the address from Min, I tried hard to remember it without writing it down, and I noticed a shadow following me. At first I thought I had to break out magic in full view of anyone who might be innocently walking by, but then I realized it was nothing magic could ever make go away. It was Blake.

I hung up with Min and stood at my car with my hand on the door handle. "Yes?" I snapped.

"I'm going with you," Blake said.

"What for?"

"Call it a hunch. A detective never ignores a hunch."

I rolled my eyes.

"You don't even know where I'm going."

"You said the orphanage."

"Yes, but I didn't say what orphanage or where. I could taking you on a wild goose chase to parts unknown," I said, hoping he'd reconsider.

"It's the Wonder Falls Orphanage on County Road 57 and Cline, right?" he said as if that was the hottest spot in town and everyone who was anyone knew about that orphanage. The twinkle in his tired eyes also let me know he was enjoying this a little.

I opened the driver's door. "How did you know?"

"I'm a detective. It's my job to know things."

I could have sworn he was trying to tell me he knew a few things about yours truly as well. I gave him a scowl and got in behind the wheel. Leaning over, I unlocked the passenger side door, and Blake climbed in. I couldn't be sure because I wouldn't give him the satisfaction of looking in his direction, but I thought he was smiling.

25. House of Records

M uch to my dismay, Blake knew exactly how to get to the orphanage, and it was set pretty far off the beaten path. The building wasn't surrounded by lush trees or wildflowers or even a forlorn playground, long rusted over from disuse. That was what I had envisioned when Min told me where he was. Nope. This place was in the rougher part of town that was full of buildings sporting plywood windows and address numbers sprayed on with black spray paint.

At that hour of the morning, the neighborhood wasn't bad, but I felt the residue of negativity from the night before. I caught sight of an alley cat skulking around the corner of a brick building. It had a few jagged edges to its ears as though it had been in its fair share of fights.

"I recognize that smell." The thought from the alley cat came to me clearly. *"You are with that animal that likes to sneak around where he doesn't belong. I taught him a lesson once to stay out of this part of town. If he comes back, I'll do it again."*

Treacle. This cat knew Treacle.

"From the looks of things, there's plenty of food and space for all you strays. Why worry yourself over one more cat?" I hoped my thoughts sounded confident even if I was worried. I'd never had a cat, stray or domestic, intrude on my thoughts so hard.

The feline watched me with slow and lazily blinking yellow eyes. *"You just make sure to tell him, or he'll look very different next time you see him. And it won't be just a scratch on his forehead."*

I gasped.

"What is it?" Blake asked.

"Oh, nothing." I coughed quickly. "For a minute, I thought I saw a rat."

I looked at the cat once more but said nothing. I'd have a long talk with Treacle about the dangers of slumming, but I knew it wouldn't do any good. The streets were his home. That sounded like a bad rap lyric.

"Is this it?" I asked, looking at a very nondescript red brick building that looked more like an abandoned bank than a place that had, at one time, housed children with no parents.

"Yup. It is."

"You don't think there are still children in there, do you?" I asked, my heart ready to sink if he said yes.

"Not at all. This place hasn't been in operation for some time. But it doesn't seem to be completely deserted."

"What makes you say that?" I was afraid he was going to say he'd seen some ghostly apparition in a window or something equally creepy. Being a witch didn't make me feel any safer from those mysterious things that go bump in the night, and even with the sun shining, I felt a shiver run up my spine.

"There are half a dozen cars in the parking lot." Blake jerked his chin toward the right of the building.

For sure, in a small parking lot surrounded by a chain link fence were a handful of cars. One of those cars was Min's. It was hard to miss the silver Mercedes, especially in this neighborhood.

Then some movement at the front of the building caught my eye. When I looked, I saw Min waving to us near the front door. He looked excited as he thrust his hands into his pockets. He must've gotten there just before Blake.

As happy as Min looked, I could tell he was wondering what Blake was doing with me.

"I just thought I'd tag along. I hope it isn't a problem." Blake said. His eyes seemed to be searching every door, window, sidewalk grate, car, and garbage can that fell into his line of vision. His eyes finally settled on Min.

It was obvious that after Min had been a suspect in the deadly explosion of the Brew-Ha-Ha that had killed our cook, he and Blake would never be anything more than civil to each other. I couldn't blame Min. Blake was a jerk and hadn't held back when he interrogated Min. Blake had stuck to the rules, used his bullying tactics, and seemed to have the strangest ability to make people feel nervous around him even if they didn't do anything.

But to his credit, he was dedicated and willing to turn every stone, even if it kept him up for days at a time. And sometimes, when the light hit him the right way, he looked handsome. But then he would open his mouth and ruin everything.

Min shook his head at Blake then focused on me. "Cath, I think this place is just what I was looking for. A diamond in the rough."

"Well, it's not an orphanage anymore, right?" I asked. "There aren't any children here?"

"No. The last child that was adopted at this facility went home with his new family back in the 1960s."

"So what is this place?"

"Well, it's become sort of the Wonder Falls house of records." He grinned again as we made our way up the steps, and Min held the door open for us.

As soon as I stepped inside, I was hit by a very familiar smell from my childhood. It was the smell of old carpet and paper. I had grown up when carbon copies were just starting to be replaced by Xerox, and my school had smelled like this place. Tons of paper and a swatch of carpet big enough to sit on for story time. It was a weird smell but one I never forgot. But on top of that, the air shifted. I couldn't quite put my finger on it, but I could tell something was there that wanted to be noticed.

Had I been with Aunt Astrid and Bea, I would have leaned in and asked if they felt it too. But looking at Blake, who acted as if his head was on a swivel so he could look in all directions, I leaned a little in the opposite direction and kept my interpretations to myself.

"House of records?" I asked, knowing I looked confused. Then I heard another loud voice.

"Good morning!"

It was an unfamiliar voice but a friendly one. Even Min jumped a little at the startling greeting. Blake stood still and stoic.

"My name is Riley. I'm the custodian of this building. Is there anything I can help you with? Needless to say we don't get many visitors, so this is a surprise." He smiled cheerfully, his fat cheeks pushing his eyes into the shape of crescent moons.

Min stepped up and introduced us all. In a quick couple of words, he asked to speak to the chief administrator.

"Well, Detective Samberg, is there a problem?" Riley looked intrigued, as if he were hoping there might be some kind of scandal in the making and, for a moment, forgot about Min and me.

"Not at all. It's really Mr. Parks who is here to inquire about the building."

"Oh, I see." Riley noticeably deflated a little, but within a few seconds, his cheery demeanor was back. "That would be Madeline Molitor. She's down the hallway this way." Riley led us down a lonely corridor. Our footsteps echoed throughout the building. "Are you looking to buy?"

"Min is a local boy who's looking to do a little good in his hometown," I bragged, making Min's cheeks color a little as he smiled.

"Is that so? That's mighty nice of you," Riley said. "I don't know what you'd want with the old place. It's long been forgotten. A skeleton crew comes in to turn the lights on and off, chase the spiders away, and keep the records in order."

"What kind of records?" I asked.

"Well, there are the documents of every adoption of course. But the new City Hall building that was built in 1999 was constructed without an insulated basement, so all the town records from there were put into these file cabinets. You've got marriage licenses, death certificates, building permit requests, traffic tickets, building permits, property lines. You name it, the paperwork is probably here."

"Is that so?" I said, trying not to tip off Blake as to what I was thinking of doing there.

"Yup. One stray spark or lightning strike here, and almost one hundred years of documented history would be gone with the wind. No one would even know what they lost."

"Why don't they put everything in a computer? It takes no time at all to scan these kinds of things," Min said, obviously adding it to the growing list of possibilities in his head.

"Well, I think you'll have to talk to Miss Molitor about that." Riley gave us all a wink and opened an old wooden door that had Administration stenciled in black letters across the frosted glass.

Inside, four gray-haired old women looked up from their desks as if they hadn't seen anyone under the age of sixty... ever.

"Miss Molitor's office is back there," Riley said, pointing toward the back of the room. "Good morning, ladies."

They all gave him a variety of greetings from spunky to grumbly. Min took the bull by the horns and strolled confidently to the back of the room and rapped firmly on the door Riley had indicated. I followed Min as Blake left with Mr. Riley. I hoped Blake wouldn't go on snooping. I wanted to find out what was going on with the death and desecration as much as he did, but a selfish part of me wanted to solve the case without anyone else's help. If Blake had the same idea to snoop in the records, he might find the Thompson records before me. But he'd have to do it the old-fashioned way. If I got my chance, a little witchcraft might help the medicine go down.

"Come!" was the greeting that came from behind the door.

Min pulled the door open and allowed me to enter first. Miss Molitor was a tiny woman who looked over a hundred. Her hair was permed into tight little gray curls. She wore glasses with decorative gold frames and garish pink lipstick that I'd bet was super popular in the fifties, when she was a newlywed or just started working outside the home or something.

Min began speaking instantly and didn't stop until Madeline Molitor was smiling and patting his hand as she shared the excitement of his plans to help preserve this amazing building. Under any other circumstances, I would have been Min's cheerleader, but I was distracted by the idea that I could very well be sitting just a couple of feet from the documents that might crack the case wide open. So I showed my support another way, and that was by asking a question.

"As things stand now, Miss Molitor, are people able to come and review these records? Say, if they were writing a report or tracing a family tree?"

"Not likely. The majority of the documents are in rows and rows of metal filing cabinets in the basement. We only manage material from the last three years on the main floor."

She barely looked at me as she spoke. I could tell she wasn't very interested in what I was asking. She was much more interested in dealing with Min. Obviously she was from that older generation of women who, if given the choice, preferred to talk business with the man. Well, he was the one with the money, and I was the one trying to snoop, and since I wasn't going to get very far with Miss Molitor, I began searching for plan B. I found it almost instantly.

Blake came back with Riley. The two of them looked as though they'd had a nice long talk together. From his expression, I was pretty sure Blake didn't have the same idea of riffling through the records as I did. I let out a sigh over that.

"Well, I'm really grateful for your time, Miss Molitor," Min said.

"Please, call me Madeline. I hope to hear from you again soon, Mr. Parks. You have some wonderful ideas. I'm not promising anything, but let's talk again soon," the old woman said.

26. Hatching a Plan

B ack at the Brew-Ha-Ha, I enjoyed an iced green tea and a turkey sandwich that Bea threw together for me. I told her how we discovered the orphanage and how we paid it a little visit.

"So you spent the morning with Blake."

I nearly choked. "Gosh, Bea! It wasn't like that. I didn't even want him to, but he insisted on tagging along." I spoke with my mouth full of food, totally ignoring any etiquette in order to set the record straight. "Just because you and Jake are back being all lovey-dovey doesn't mean the rest of us are interested in catching that bug."

Bea smiled as a guilty blush rose to her cheeks. I was happy for her. This was how things should be.

"Hey, since you guys are all back on better footing, I have a favor to ask."

"Anything, sister. You know that."

I shrugged my shoulders up to my ears and squinted. "Well, maybe you should hear what it is first."

Bea looked at me with her right eyebrow arching high up on her forehead while she crossed her arms. Just then, Aunt Astrid entered from the back kitchen.

"Aunt Astrid, I'll need you too."

She looked a little startled as if she had been deep in thought. We made our way to the cellar to have a private conversation, and I revealed my genius idea.

"You're talking about breaking and entering," Bea said calmly. "I don't know how Jake would be able to help us with that."

"Actually, it would just be entering. I noticed a window on the first floor without a mesh screen or bars, and as luck would have it, the lock wasn't in place. All we'd need to do is get up to it and push," I said proudly, as if I had just recited the capitals of every state. But the looks I got from Bea and Aunt Astrid made it seem as if I had just recited the filthiest limerick ever penned.

"And where is this place located?" Aunt Astrid asked with slow, deliberate words.

I gave the address, and both women threw up their arms.

"Are you kidding?" and "You've lost your mind" came out of their mouths at the same time.

"That part of town is a demilitarized zone. Are you serious? Jake has told me about what kinds of things the beat cops over there have had to deal with. To say it isn't safe is an understatement." Bea put her hands on her hips. "I can't tell him anything about this. He'd hit the roof."

"So you're in?" I said, grinning slyly.

"I don't know. Mom?"

Aunt Astrid stared into space for a moment. Then, looking at me with twinkling eyes, she said, "Unfortunately, Cath is right to think we might find the answer there. And even if Blake had put two and two together and seen the importance of those records, he would get them by the book, and that could take days, if not weeks. Who else will get hurt in that amount of time?" She pulled the hem of her dress up as she ascended the cellar stairs back into the Brew-Ha-Ha. "Bea, you'll stay home. Cath and I will go."

"Wait. What?" Bea looked a little let down.

Aunt Astrid stopped climbing. "With you and Jake just getting things back on track, you don't need to steer yourself off a cliff by breaking the law with us. Besides, we'll need a connection inside the WFPD if we get pinched."

"You just used the word 'pinched' like the short guy in that one mob movie," I said, looking Aunt Astrid up and down.

"Be at my house at eleven thirty. We'll leave at midnight," she said and disappeared up the stairs.

Bea took my hand and looked at me sternly. "Be careful. And if Jake finds out… I'll deny I knew anything about it."

I chuckled a little as I squeezed her hand. But inside, my nerves were full of electricity.

That night, before I left to pick up Aunt Astrid, I had a long talk with Treacle. Actually, Treacle had a long talk with me. It seemed word got around in the feline world, just as it did in the human world.

"That just isn't a safe place for people to go," he said.

"I saw that. And I saw what kind of strays you're dealing with. That doesn't make me very happy either," I replied.

That wasn't what he wanted to hear, and he sat with his head and neck stretched up tall and his tail whipping back and forth. *It isn't just that. Those places are everywhere. They have a sickness. Like a rabies. And sometimes you can catch something.*

We aren't going to move there, I reassured him. *We're going to get into that building and research the records then hurry up and come home. That's all.*

The only thing on Treacle that moved was his tail. He was not happy. Finally he stood, stretched, and trotted off toward the open bedroom window. Hopping up on the sill, he turned and looked at me. *Be careful.*

Yes, you too. Come back home tomorrow, and we'll have breakfast. Smoked salmon?

He licked his whiskers but said nothing and was again out into the darkness. I looked at the clock and realized it was time to go. Aunt Astrid would be waiting.

27. Breaking and Entering

T he idea of breaking into a government building and rummaging through some records had been enough to keep me flighty and distracted all day, but when I pulled up to the house, Astrid was asleep on her front porch swing, a pink, floral decorative pillow snugly wrapped in her arms. Waking her up was like poking a grizzly bear with a stick.

"Come on," I whispered, hoping no insomnia sufferer was watching us. "We've got to get moving."

Finally, after she gave some low grumbles and growls, her eyes flickered open and she smiled. "What are we waiting for?" She walked briskly down the front porch steps to my car and got in.

I hadn't seen her that excited and animated in quite some time.

We drove to the orphanage in relative silence. I knew Aunt Astrid was mumbling a protection spell over us as we drove, and one of the perks was that every light turned green in our favor. But as the neighborhood began to turn, the sad, frumpy place I had seen in the morning transformed into a sinister maze of streets with jagged shadows and unseen eyes from pitch-black windows.

"Are you all right to do this?" I asked.

"Never better," she said, smiling.

"This… I don't get… is this something on your bucket list or something?" I asked. My head went back and forth between the road and Aunt Astrid. "To break a major law, commit a halfway serious offense before you pass into the great beyond? Because I'm starting to think you're enjoying this a little too much. Usually I'm the one taking unnecessary chances."

"I can't help it," Astrid said. "I find it exhilarating."

She laughed, and I shook my head. We drove for just a little longer until we came up to Cline Street.

"Well, my stomach is in knots, so let's get this over with. That's the building just up ahead. I think we should park a little bit away from the building, but that means if we get into any trouble, we'll have to run."

Suddenly, Aunt Astrid's face became serious. "There's a protection spell already on that building." She spoke in a quiet voice as if she didn't want the building to hear her. "And it isn't a friendly one."

I stopped the car about a block away and turned off the ignition. My chest got a lot tighter. Maybe I should have told Blake my idea and waited the couple of weeks for a warrant. "Can we get through it?"

"Yes. It's been there for a while and is pretty thin and worn. But be prepared for a little nausea. It isn't a white protection spell."

Goose bumps rose on my arms, and I shivered. We got out of the car and looked around suspiciously. Cat burglars we were not. Laurel and Hardy... well, maybe.

"The open window is on the southwest side of the building," I whispered. "Just around that corner."

As soon as we set foot on the property line, I felt it, a shift in the air that made it smell a little like metal. We stuck to the shadows as we inched our way around the building.

"I didn't notice this during the day," I whispered.

"You wouldn't have. It is a nocturnal spell designed to protect…"

"The building?" I asked nervously.

"The contents of the building."

"So you think the records might have more information than we first thought?"

"I'm not sure it's protecting the records at all."

I swallowed hard. Finally, I saw the right window. With just a little elbow grease, it slid right up. Cigarette butts littered the sill and the ground outside the window. Someone was obviously too set in their ways to adhere to the strict no-smoking policies implemented in every government building.

I gave Aunt Astrid a boost, and she shimmied into the open window with such grace that if I didn't know her, I would have thought she had been doing it her whole life. She helped pull me up.

As I had predicted, the office was creepy and scary in the darkness. It was just an office with desks and files and not a whole lot more, yet I got the feeling that weird things roamed the halls at night.

"Where are the records?" she asked.

"Miss Molitor said they were in the basement."

"Let's go." Aunt Astrid pulled a small LED flashlight from her pocket. It cut through the darkness and illuminated millions of little dust particles swirling in the air.

We exited the office and tiptoed down the hallway, checking each door until we found one at the very end of the corridor that read STAIRS. With a deep breath, I pulled the door open. It squeaked terribly, echoing throughout the building.

"Hasn't been opened in a while, I guess," I said, trying to calm my nerves.

Aunt Astrid gasped. Her flashlight shined on nothing other than stairs, but she obviously felt something.

"Let's hurry," she said, making her way down the stairs one step at a time, carefully holding on to the railing.

At the bottom, there were two more doors. One read Boiler Room. The other said nothing. We entered the nameless door.

I barely noticed Aunt Astrid had been mumbling almost the entire time we came down the stairs. Finally I looked at her face in the eerie glow of the flashlight and saw her sorting through the layers of the past to hopefully zero in on what we were looking for.

"There." She pointed at an olive green filing cabinet with at least an inch of dust on top of it.

I walked up to it and pointed at the top drawer. She shook her head. The second drawer was also a no. Finally, Aunt Astrid indicated the bottom drawer. I sat on the dirty floor, yanked open the drawer with a metallic *clink, clank zzshronk*.

There it was. The file stood out as if it had been waiting for us to find it.

Thompson Family: 1808 – 2009

The file was thick with birth certificates and death certificates for dozens of obscure branches stretching out from their family tree. Names that were familiar in town but faces I just couldn't remember. One thing jumped out at me so suddenly, I felt as if I had been slapped.

"We have to get going," Aunt Astrid hissed urgently.

"I don't believe this." My mind couldn't focus. I was shaking and felt a chill run up my spine.

"Cath!" Her voice sounded scared. "We've got to go! Now!"

"Should I take the file?" I was tripping over my thoughts and didn't know what to do. It was like one of those dreams where I was struggling to run but my legs just wouldn't move.

"No! Put it back! Put everything back! We need to get out of this building now!"

Finally my head clicked, and I heard her loud and clear. Stuffing the folder back where it belonged, I shut the drawer and jumped to my feet. Just then, we froze. We heard noises. I quickly tiptoed next to my aunt and held her hand. We stood there for what felt like an eternity. I watched her face as she sorted through the dimensions of the future and past and everything else in between. Her grip became tighter until I wasn't sure if it was *our* present where we were hearing noises or something in another dimension trying to bust its way through to this one. It seemed to be all around us and even, I shuddered to think it, inside us, echoing in our heads.

"Let's go!" I pulled Aunt Astrid toward the stairs.

I thought I might have to help her get up the stairs, but to my surprise and relief, she shot up them like a bullet. We burst through the wooden door into the dark hallway and pressed our backs against the cold concrete wall. Both of us held our breath.

Something was pursuing us. Something big and diabolical was rattling the foundation of the building.

"It was down there with us," Aunt Astrid said in a terrified whisper. "I think it's coming up the stairs."

Reluctantly, I pressed my ear against the wood door. As sure as the stars were in the sky that night, I heard the footsteps. I heard the breathing. I heard the growling.

This time it was Aunt Astrid who grabbed my hand and pulled me back toward the office. Once inside it, we quickly shut the door and ran to the window that, thankfully, was still open.

While Aunt Astrid backed her way out onto the safety of the pavement, I felt my body shake with fear. This had to be how the men floating around the sunken USS *Indianapolis* felt while being rescued as sharks continued to attack them from below.

I wouldn't turn around. I wouldn't look at the office door for fear of what I might see. But I knew whatever it was had crawled up from the basement. It had moved up the stairs with slow, deliberate steps, and now it was making its way down the hall.

"Hurry," I urged my aunt. "Please."

She nodded and grunted as she swung her second leg over the sill and hopped down. Looking around quickly, she saw nothing and waved to me. "Come on, Cath. Hurry."

She didn't have to tell me twice. But against my better judgment, against my gut instinct, against my own will, I turned and looked at the wooden door with Administration stenciled across it.

A ghoulish face, distorted by the glass, grinned a sadistic grin at me as its red eyes burned into mine.

I dove out the window, slamming it shut behind me, and onto the hard pavement, where I scraped up my palms and tore a nice size hole in my favorite black jeans.

"Are you all right?" Aunt Astrid asked as she yanked me to my feet and pulled me toward the car. Had I broken a leg, she would have continued to drag me away from that place, all the while soothing and encouraging as she was doing. "It's okay. We're all right now. The car is just up ahead. Come on, honey. Let's keep going."

Once inside the car, I locked the doors, started the engine, and peeled out of there under the blurry gaze of a couple of men sharing a drink from a paper bag.

Only once I saw the cheery sight of Aunt Astrid's front porch did I let out a sigh. It seemed as if I might have been holding my breath for the entire drive.

"Can I…"

"Sleep overnight here?" Aunt Astrid finished my sentence. "Absolutely."

I sighed with relief. "Thanks."

We didn't say too much about what we had heard. I didn't tell Aunt Astrid about the face I had seen. I would wait until the sun came up and Bea was with us. The hustle and bustle of a normal day under a normal sun could chase away the shadows and boogeymen.

28. The Park Family Secret

"I stayed awake all night waiting for the phone to ring. I was sure I'd get a call from Jake telling me my mom and cousin had been picked up for breaking into a government building," Bea said, pouring hot tea into our cups the following morning in Aunt Astrid's kitchen.

"You have no idea," I said, wrapping my hands around the warm mug.

"Did you find out anything?"

Aunt Astrid sipped her tea and looked at me. I hadn't told her what I'd read in the documents on the Thompson family. I felt a little guilty even mentioning it. It was obviously something that was intended to stay buried.

"Yes," I said, looking back at Aunt Astrid.

"So? Don't keep me waiting." Bea's eyes bounced back and forth between us.

"There was something there. Something that knew we were there and wasn't very happy," Aunt Astrid said.

"What happened?"

Aunt Astrid told Bea in great detail what had happened while I had my back to her as I read the complete Thompson file. She saw people coming and going, heard conversations about the building and the files, and she also saw where the protection spell had come from.

"Topher?" Bea gasped, looking at me.

"This is the first I'm hearing about this too," I said, shaking my head in disbelief. When we had gotten back to Aunt Astrid's place, we were so shocked and exhausted that sleep overcame us almost instantly. Even if we had wanted to talk about what had happened, our minds just wouldn't allow it.

"I'm not sure why but…" Aunt Astrid shook her head and pulled an apple pie, with one slice missing, out of her refrigerator. With three graceful movements, she swept up three rose-decorated small plates, pulled three forks from the copper canister on the counter, and snagged the pie server from the cutlery drawer.

"Well, I'm not sure what to make of this, but from what I saw in the file, that may not be so hard to believe." I took another sip of tea as a heaping slice of apple pie made its way in front of me.

Pulling her chair up to the kitchen table, Aunt Astrid took a seat.

"There was a birth certificate in there. Well, there were lots of them throughout the years and nothing strange, nothing out of order except…" I felt as though I was gossiping, and that was bad enough, but I saw no other way to help get this situation under control. "I saw Thomas Thompson born to mother Alice Thompson and father…"

Bea's back straightened, and her eyes widened.

"Lei Park. Min's father."

"What?" Bea and Aunt Astrid cried at once.

"Hey, I'm not saying it's true. I'm saying that that's what was on the birth certificate. But why would it be there if it wasn't true? I mean, the whole thing is really messed up, right?"

"Min's father was Tommy Thompson's father too?" Bea exclaimed. "How could that be?"

"Well, the certificate didn't go into details, but I'm guessing that when they were younger, Mr. Park and Miss Thompson had a fling that resulted in a child." I shoveled a huge scoop of apple pie into my mouth so I wouldn't have to say any more.

"Well, duh, that's what happened," Bea said. "But something like that would have gotten around. People would have heard about it. This is a small town, and gossip tumbles from mouths as easily as the water down the waterfall."

"That is a beautiful comparison," I said, giving Bea a wink.

"Thank you. But still, don't you think someone would have spoken about this before?"

"People can keep secrets if they choose to. It's just that so many people choose not to," Aunt Astrid said.

"If that's true, then it might explain why Topher seemed so agitated at the play," I said, thinking hard while cutting myself another piece of pie.

"What are you talking about?" Aunt Astrid asked.

"The play. You guys were in your seats when I was in the back with Min and Blake. Topher came galloping along with his britches in a bunch, calling Min all kinds of names. It makes a little more sense that he'd have some animosity toward the men in the Park family."

"But Topher was never rude to them before. He might be a bit on the eccentric side but never hurtful," Bea insisted and sipped her tea.

"Right, but now he's got an Unfamiliar attached to him, feeding him lies and pulling him down into that darkness where who knows what worms its way into his mind," I said. "Maybe thirty years ago, he did hate Lei Park or everyone in the Park family for this indiscretion but came to terms with it. If there was still just a sliver of resentment, that creature would find it and infect it until it became a consuming cancer."

"And all the while making it look like Old Murray was the problem." Aunt Astrid nodded. "All along, that Unfamiliar had its vise grip on Topher and—"

"Pointed out to Topher that someone in the Park family was a closer living relation to Alice than anyone else in town. If he gets his hands on Min, or preferably Lei Park, then raising the dead and giving life to the Unfamiliar will probably work." I swallowed hard as I thought about the face I'd seen staring back at me through the frosted glass at the orphanage.

"What?" Bea asked. "Your face just went pale."

I wasn't sure if I should say anything about it. Maybe I hadn't even seen it. Maybe I had just gotten wrapped up in the moment and my mind was playing tricks on me. Maybe it was a result of the old spell hanging over that place like webbing.

"When we were getting out of that building, I saw something," I said.

"The Unfamiliar," Aunt Astrid said as if she already knew.

I looked at her with wide eyes. "How did you know?"

"I caught a glimpse of it moving through time. It rips the fabric of the dimensions like it's going through paper."

"What was it doing hanging out at an old government building that practically no one ever visits?" Bea asked.

"That I don't know," Aunt Astrid said. "But I knew we stirred it up just a few minutes after I was shown where the files that might help us were. I just thought we could get out of there before it made it through to our dimension. I guess I was wrong."

I shivered. Even with the comfort of the sun and the protection of my family around me, I felt vulnerable, as if I was only wearing a towel and had to go slay a dragon.

"Does that mean the Unfamiliar sometimes detaches itself from Topher?" Bea asked, pushing her empty plate aside.

Aunt Astrid walked to her pantry and opened the door, revealing not just canned goods and baking supplies but three shelves filled with books. The one she retrieved was a small black leather-bound thing with fingerprints in flour on the cover. The pages inside were yellowed and almost transparent with age. She peeled them away from each other delicately, one at a time. "According to this..."

"What is that one? I don't think I've ever seen it," I said, peeking at the writing.

"This is sort of like the Cliff's Notes on Unfamiliars," Aunt Astrid said, her brow wrinkling over her nose. "It won't tell us how to get rid of the little bugger, but it will tell us its schedule."

I looked at Bea, who shook her head and shrugged.

"The Unfamiliar is strongest during the full moon, but last night was two nights *before* the full moon. It was weak, and Topher must have either pushed it out of his mind or was so exhausted when he fell asleep that it couldn't get through to him. We can assume it whispers to him incessantly, driving him crazy one word at a time."

"That poor man," Bea said. "He needs a healing spell, but it's no good to do one until the Unfamiliar is gone."

"So it came sniffing around for us. It knows we're here. It knows what we are. And it isn't scared." Aunt Astrid had barely touched her pie.

I finished my second slice of pie and washed it down with the remaining tea, which had gone lukewarm. "Well, it's going to be up to something tonight. My gut is telling me that we need to let the Parks know they're in danger."

"How are you going to do that?" Bea asked. "Do you realize how crazy our story would sound? Not to mention how embarrassing for them? There's no easy way to address the issue."

"No, there isn't. You want to do it?" I asked, looking at Bea with puppy dog eyes.

She put her hands up in front of her and shook her head. "No way. I'm getting my own house in order before I butt in on anyone else. Besides, you're the one Min has eyes for. It would be better coming from someone he knows and cares for."

"Has eyes for?" I felt my cheeks flash hot pink. "What are you talking about?"

"Oh, nothing." Bea folded her arms across her chest and snickered.

Marshmallow jumped into Aunt Astrid's lap, hopped up on the table, and made herself comfortable there.

"Treacle was here this morning. He looked like he had gotten into a little scuffle," Marshmallow said to me.

"I'm sure he did," I said. *"Did he say where he had been or where he was going?"*

"He didn't want you to see him the way he looked, so I assume he was going to the shelter for a quick cleanup from Cody and Old Murray before you could see him."

"Oh, that little sneak. Thanks for the tip." I scratched Marshmallow behind the ears, starting her purr engine.

"Sure, but you didn't hear it from me."

Bea and Aunt Astrid didn't hear my conversation with Marshmallow, but I think they could tell something was up.

"I'm going to go get this thing with the Parks over with," I said. "It isn't something that needs to be put off any longer. Plus, if it is the full moon the night after tomorrow, we have to be prepared."

Again, I thought of that thing that had grinned at me. It suddenly wasn't as scary as what I had to tell the Parks. I thought what I needed to do was walk off the two slices of pie

I had just eaten while I came up with a script that would prompt the Parks without revealing the whole story.

Leaving Aunt Astrid and Bea to discuss the plan for the evening, I drove to the animal shelter to pick up Treacle. I'd drop him off at home with a little food and a stern talking-to, then I'd head off to the Parks' house.

29. Monsters Under the Bed

The shelter was several healthy blocks away, and with the sun shining on my face and just a kiss of a breeze blowing through the trees and carrying the smell of mimosa, I was feeling better. I knew I still had a lot of work ahead of me in the next few hours, but I was beginning to feel like I could handle it. Come what may, I'd make it through, along with the other Greenstones.

But as I caught sight of the sign for the shelter, something inside me started to doubt my success. And not just success in talking with the Parks but everything. Suddenly the sun was covered by storm clouds and the flowers wilted. I knew it wasn't really happening, but it felt like it was, way deep down in my soul. Not realizing my pace had slowed down, I felt as though maybe I should turn around.

"Treacle is in there. At least, I think he is. I can't just leave him," I said, my steps getting smaller and smaller.

The thought of my cat made me square my shoulders and pick up my pace. If I got hurt, that was one thing. But if something thought of hurting my cat, well, that was just plain cruel. I wasn't about to leave Treacle just because of a few woogie-boogie feelings.

I tried to focus and call his name with my thoughts, but I couldn't get through. Something was blocking my thoughts. Now my steps really quickened, until I was almost running up the sidewalk to the front entrance. Before I could even get my hand on the front door handle, I heard yelling.

It sounded like a poker game gone bad. I instantly recognized Cody telling someone to just calm down. I heard a female voice saying she was sorry and didn't understand. It sounded like Naomi LaChance. She had been stopping in regularly to check on Topher while Cody worked at the shelter, probably because she still felt attached to Tommy.

A million thoughts went through my head as my hand touched the door handle, took hold, and pulled it open. I took two steps inside. Cody was saying he was sorry over and over. He and Naomi were cornered and looking at an old man, who had his back to me as I walked in.

"What's going on?" I asked, a little out of breath. I heard Treacle calling me from the back room. In my mind, I answered him, but he kept calling and talking too fast for me to understand what he was saying.

"Cath. Oh jeez, you might want to go and get Chief Talbot or Jake or someone to come over here right away." Cody's eyes looked at me then darted back to the old man who still had his back to me.

"Now, Topher, you need to just calm down. I don't know what your issue is, but we can help if you'll just relax a bit." Naomi's voice was barely any calmer than Cody's. She was visibly shaking.

"Topher, come on, man. You and me are friends. There's no need to get mad. I don't even know what I said. I just..." Cody stumbled over his words, his eyes wide and scared.

Topher was blocking the door and preventing me from getting any farther in the room. I looked at his hands and didn't see a weapon, but his fists were clenching and unclenching in a menacing and deliberate manner. There were papers and a broken potted plant on the floor, along with an overturned waiting room chair, and I saw a new crack in the plaster of the front reception desk.

"Hey, Topher," I said in a quiet voice. "It's me, Cath Greenstone. What's going on here?"

His head tilted a little in my direction as if he was listening, but he didn't turn around. Everyone stood still. Not a sound came from any of us until Topher spoke. Or at least the words came from his mouth. I don't think it was really him talking.

"I know you," he said. "I know you are still afraid of monsters under your bed."

The words struck me dumb, and before I could utter anything, the old man spun around to face me. It was Topher's body and face, but something was working just below the surface. My eyes blurred, as if I was viewing a photo taken in mid-movement or perhaps filtered through a frosted window.

The temperature in the room dropped at least twenty degrees, and I was paralyzed with fear. I wanted to run, but the thought of Treacle in his cage held me there. With Cody and Naomi just as scared as me, well, someone had to stand up to it.

"Under the bed," it hissed again.

The evil smile fell from his face, and the Unfamiliar looked at me seriously. Before I could call out a binding spell or even a simple hex to numb his legs, the old man rushed to me and pushed me into the wall, where my head snapped back and thudded against the fake wood paneling. Out the door he went. I didn't dare chase him.

"What was that all about?" Naomi asked. "He was as pleasant as punch all day until he started talking to you." She elbowed Cody, who looked at her apologetically.

He was just a kid compared to the rest of us. Compared to the Unfamiliar, he was just a baby who it could easily frighten.

"I don't know," Cody said, sitting on one of the waiting room chairs and running his hands over his short dark hair. His eyes looked worried as if he might be in trouble.

I rubbed the back of my own head and sat next to Cody. "What were you guys doing?" I tried to act as baffled as they were even though I knew the thing that was hiding there in the old man's body.

"I just brought him over to get a little fresh air," Naomi said. "While Old Murray is still recovering and taking it easy, Topher doesn't have anyone, really, to look out for him except for Cody. So I've been stopping by his place. I asked if he wanted to take a walk and see Cody."

"And he was okay with that?" I asked, still trying to remain calm.

"Yeah. We walked here, and Cody brought him out a little cup of water and told him that he went to visit Old Murray," Naomi continued, still standing in the same spot as if she was afraid to move.

I put my hand on Cody's shoulder. "How's he doing?" I hoped Cody couldn't feel my nerves trembling.

"He's doing great. That's what I told Topher. I told him how good the old man was doing, thanks to Bea's alternative medicine and what the doctors did for him, then I said I saw Mr. Park, and it was like someone flipped a switch, right?" He looked at Naomi, who was nodding as she swept a couple of stray strands of long black hair away from her face and nervously tucked them into the bun she was wearing.

"Lei Park stopped by to see Old Murray?" I asked, hoping maybe I wouldn't have to pay a visit to the Parks' residence.

"No, no. I meant Min Park. He's a mister too, you know."

I nodded. That made more sense. Min was that kind of person.

"It just sent Topher off the deep end. He started knocking things over and yelling out all kinds of gibberish that made no sense. Then he was saying things like, 'If it doesn't work with him, I'll try you next. The both of you. The both of you.'" Cody looked at Naomi again.

"What is that, like, dementia? Could he be having a breakdown after living all those years by himself out in the woods?" Naomi asked, picking up some of the papers on the floor.

"Uh, yeah. Well, it could be." I couldn't tell them that it was more than likely not even Topher talking, but some really annoyed, really nasty demon with a yearning for a strong, young, previously deceased body to dress up in and roam the streets looking for more lives to ruin.

"I'll get you Treacle. He moseyed in this morning looking a little worn. I think he got into a fight." Cody slowly walked to the back door with the word CATS in thick black block letters with a silhouette of a cat underneath it.

He emerged carrying my big black cat, and I instantly saw the small clip out of his right ear.

"Oh, Treacle, what have you been getting into?" I said, scooping the cat into my arms and holding him tightly. He had been scared, and so had I. His motor started to run, and the purring felt comforting as he nuzzled into my neck. "If you could put this on my running tab?" I joked. It seemed as if I was always paying the shelter a fee for my cat. "Are you two going to be all right? Do you want me to send Chief Talbot over, you know, just for the heck of it?"

Cody and Naomi shook their heads.

"I'm going to see my grandpa again tonight. I'll ask him what he thinks we should do," Cody said.

"Good idea," I said.

All we needed was a few more hours, and we might be able to help Topher without police intervention. I hoped. But now I still had to get to the Parks. If just the mention of the Park name sent Topher off like that, only heaven knew what he would do if he actually got his hands on one of them.

30. Park House

Stepping foot into Min's parents' house was not only like stepping back in time to my teenage years but to an exotic and mysterious place. Beautiful Korean paintings graced the walls. The furniture was sparse but elegantly arranged. Lush green plants grew from baskets and pots placed all over the house, giving the atmosphere a natural, organic feel. Family photos of Min growing up were scattered around in abundance.

At the front door was a row of shoes, including a pair of size nine black ballet flats that were mine. It was customary in Asian homes to take off your shoes even before closing the door. The home was a sanctuary. It was a peaceful place for contemplation and meditation. Usually. But not today.

Mrs. Park seemed civil, while Mr. Park was cold and standoffish as usual. I tried not to take it personally. I told them why I'd come. It seemed they knew exactly what I was talking about when I said I'd come to warn them about Topher's behavior while pretending I knew nothing about why he might be acting that way. I thought I'd pulled it off fairly convincingly, but the Parks still seemed to assume I knew something.

It wasn't long before they started arguing. As I looked at them, Mr. Park particularly, I thought about Tommy. He hadn't looked much like Mr. Park, except for the black hair and tan skin. He must've taken after his mother. I supposed if anyone were to look closely, he could have seemed a bit Asian, but mostly, he seemed Hispanic.

"What are you trying to say?" Mrs. Park yelled at her husband, who stood straight and defiantly in their living room.

I had shrunk back into the chair I was sitting in in the kitchen, trying to figure out how to get to the front door and slip out unnoticed.

"You heard the girl," Mr. Park said in a low voice through clenched teeth. "This trouble has come back to us and now—"

"To us? This was not my trouble. You brought this with you, and now we have to explain to the whole world—"

They went on arguing for several more minutes.

"I really just think he's chosen you guys to fixate on." I'd explained how he had exploded at the theater and at the mere mention of Min's name. "I hate to say it, but you guys have a nice business in town, and everyone knows you. You know how Topher is. If we didn't grow up with him around, we'd think he was just a string of dynamite short of being the Unabomber, living up there alone in the woods and keeping so much to himself. Yeah, it's just one of those things." I tried to act naïve, but when Mrs. Park's eyes filled with tears, I knew they knew what this was about. I was pretty sure they knew I knew.

"You know what this is about, don't you?" she'd asked her husband.

"No," was all Mr. Park had said at first. But he couldn't look at his wife. Instead, he held his head up high and looked past her out the window.

That must have been something he had done before, because Mrs. Park pounced. "Yes, you do. A problem of the past has finally risen to the surface. There will be no rest until you face this shame."

"I do not need the council of a woman!" Mr. Park had barked. He got angrier and angrier by the minute. "The past cannot be changed!"

"That's true, but you can make amends. You never did that with me or with Min. You let Min think he wasn't good enough when it was you who had the indiscretion."

My whole body had heated up with embarrassment. What was I doing, sitting there with a tiny cup of tea that Mrs. Park had poured for me over fifteen minutes earlier? Had they forgotten I was sitting there? Didn't they want to know what to do next?

Apparently not, because they'd continued their argument, and I learned a little bit more about the whole situation than I really cared to know.

"What can I do now? The mother is dead," Mr. Park growled.

"Her name was Alice. You are not so cruel you have forgotten the name of the mother of your first son? Your first son, Thomas, who is also dead, not knowing his real father." Her voice was loud, and if no one in the town knew about this, there was a good chance a couple of them might know now. "You never talk to me about this. You say it happened like it was nothing. Like I was to accept it and just move on. Forgive and forget. But all this time, you never make things right. So how can I make it right? How can I clean up your mess? And when you see his name in the paper, you say nothing? You shed no tears. You don't go to the funeral? You don't mourn him?"

Those words made Mr. Park lower his head and close his eyes. "I do mourn him. You don't know this burden I have carried."

His voice was low, and I thought for a moment I would cry myself.

Mrs. Park walked up to her husband and stood directly in front of him, forcing him to make eye contact with her. For a second, I thought she was going to crack him across the face. But she didn't. She stood there strong and straight.

"How can you say that when I have carried it with you?" she asked.

"A woman's burden is not the same as a man's. There is more to this than you can possibly understand."

Mrs. Park folded her arms across her chest. "Then maybe you need to talk to Topher. Man to man. And you both can mourn and finally lay to rest this mess that you caused."

"I wouldn't suggest doing that," I said, putting my hands up and instantly regretting opening my mouth. They glared at me like I was some kind of interloper, which, at that moment, I was. "I'm not trying to get into your business. Really, I'm not. But going to talk to Topher right now may just be, well, too dangerous. You may end up doing more harm than good."

"You are not part of this family," Mr. Park said calmly but with bitterness. "I don't need advice from you."

Mrs. Park seemed to agree with her husband and looked at me with anger and hurt in her eyes. All I could think of was what Min would think of all this. What would he think of me bringing this into his family's home?

I nodded and stood, hearing the bones in my knees crack with relief. I had been sitting so stone still, they had locked up a little. "I'm sorry. But please don't go talk to Topher. He's not well. Give it a couple of days, or weeks even."

I could tell by their faces they were getting angrier by the second, and their silence was making me nervous. Images of Mrs. Park physically tossing me out of her home to land square on my keister flashed through my mind, so I made my way quickly to the front door.

They resumed their argument in Korean. I felt bad for them and for myself. Had I done the right thing by warning them? Yes. Yes, I had. They had to know that Topher wasn't stable right now.

But no matter how much I tried to comfort myself, I still felt as though I'd done way more harm than good. I wanted to call Min right away and maybe give him a heads-up about everything that had gone on, but I could only imagine what Mr. and Mrs. Park would say if I told Min about the relationship between his father and Alice Thompson.

I decided to try something new and kept my mouth shut.

I made my way back to Aunt Astrid's house. When I got there, Bea had left for the Brew-Ha-Ha and Aunt Astrid was searching around for a couple of books we needed to study to prepare for the full moon in two days.

"There is nothing you can do now, Cath. What's done is done," she said, searching through her library, which was spread throughout almost every room in her home.

"You sound like you aren't happy I went to them."

"Your intentions were good. I know they were. But this is a sticky topic. It might have been better if you'd gone over your plan with Bea and me."

I picked at my thumbnail. I didn't think anyone could make me feel worse than the Parks had, but I was wrong. Aunt Astrid was right. I should have talked it out a little more, especially after I'd seen the shape Topher was in at the animal shelter. That reminded me of something I was reluctant to talk to anyone about. When I mentioned it to Aunt Astrid, she looked at me with a frightened expression.

"He mentioned monsters under your bed?" she said, her hand to her chest and her voice quieter.

I nodded.

She quickly turned back to her books and pulled an old-looking gray tome off the shelf. When she blew on it, a few specks of dust flew off, and she hustled to another shelf across the room. She ran her index finger along the spines until an "a-ha" let me know she'd found the book she was looking for.

"Sit down," she said to me without emotion.

I sat in the corner of her soft, flower-patterned couch and looked at her. Aunt Astrid's eyes scanned around deliberately, as if she was pushing her gaze through the various dimensions that only she could see. She opened the gray book and read aloud.

When Aunt Astrid read a spell, it sounded like a song. The words were like a poem and brought a slight swirl to the air, like a gentle breeze. I felt calm settle over me. Then her voice became quieter and the words indistinguishable as she muttered them. Her hand rested gently on my head, and I felt the tingly sensation of magic float over and through me. The whole ritual took less than a minute, but I immediately felt different.

"What was that for?" I asked.

"It's just a little protection spell. That Unfamiliar looked at you. He saw your face, even if it was just through the frosted glass of that door. Today he got a good look at you. Not just your face but inside your soul. He knows more than he should. I don't know how that can be."

I didn't like how her face looked and how she wouldn't meet my gaze.

"So this spell will protect me?" I asked.

"It will make it a little hard for him to read your thoughts, but it isn't permanent nor is it foolproof. And for a short time, you may not be able to talk to the cats."

My eyes filled with tears, but I nodded my understanding.

"I'm sorry, honey, but it's the only way," Aunt Astrid said.

I knew she felt bad, but I also got the feeling I was being punished just a little bit.

31. Protection Spell

The next two days were spent preparing for the full moon as if we were all cramming for finals. This was difficult as we'd reopened the Brew-Ha-Ha already. The whole town had missed us, and we were busier than ever. We took on more staff to handle the customers. We would've rejoiced in our grand reopening if it weren't for all of this Unfamiliar trouble.

Every night after closing down the Brew-Ha-Ha, we gathered in the cellar, and while sipping herb tea, we dog-eared pages, underlined passages, made notes into the wee hours of the morning.

"Well, from everything we've read, it's pretty obvious the Parks will be the next target. They're the only family Topher has left, even if they don't acknowledge each other as such," Bea said.

"Everything in these books regarding raising the dead confirms a familial tie is the strongest way raise the dead. No wonder it's never practiced. How morbid."

"Is anyone hungry?" I asked a little sheepishly.

"Really? You're thinking of food now?" Bea looked at me while Aunt Astrid chuckled in the corner.

"Come on. We have to open the Brew-Ha-Ha in what?" I looked at my watch. "Holy moly. Forty-five minutes. I don't know about you two, but I want something a little stronger than tea to drink and something with sugar to eat."

"I think Cath is right," Astrid said. "We'll need our strength tonight. We need to eat and get some rest."

We made our way up from the cellar. The bright morning light cascaded in through the big front windows, and coffee was quickly brewed. Every morning, Daisy's Garden, the local flower shop, left a fresh delivery of flowers by the front door. I scooped them up and deeply inhaled the wonderful smell of rosebuds with sprigs of baby's breath. After breaking up the bouquet, I filled the tiny bud vases that graced the counter and the couple of mismatched tables we'd acquired during the last village-wide garage sale.

A bit of movement out of my peripheral vision caught my attention. It was Treacle. He slinked in, setting off the tinkling bells over the door. He looked at me. I looked at him. I couldn't hear a thing.

Nearly bursting into tears, I scooped him up in my arms, stroking his black fur. "I'm sorry, buddy. I can't talk right now. Not until this whole mess is over with."

I rubbed his head and felt his purring motor. I don't know if he understood me since we usually communicated telepathically. I hoped he did. I inspected his scratches from the other night. They appeared to be getting better, and for that, I was thankful. I set him on the counter, where he batted the baby's breath for a second then looked at me.

Aunt Astrid came up to the counter and skirted around it to sit at the nearest table. "Well, look who came to visit." She ran her hand over Treacle's back, making him arch his body happily.

"I can't hear him. I don't think there has ever been a time I didn't hear him talk to me."

Tilting her head to the left, Aunt Astrid smiled. "It won't last too much longer, honey. I promise. But it's better safe than sorry. You can explain to Treacle once this whole mess is over."

I nodded, my eyes still stinging as I tried to keep from crying like a baby. Then someone set off the bells over the door with a fierce push. It was Jake and Blake. Wiping my eyes, I straightened up and squared my shoulders.

"Good morning, boys. Coffee?" I said, sniffling as I smiled.

Blake looked at me as if I had turned green. He stepped a little closer and was about to say something when Jake made his announcement.

"No, Cath. We've got a problem."

Bea came up front from the kitchen. "Hi, honey." She leaned over the counter to greet Jake, who met her halfway for a kiss. "Something wrong?"

"Topher's gone missing. Have you seen him?"

Bea, Aunt Astrid, and I looked at each other, and even Treacle stood up and nudged me with his head.

"No. We haven't." I said. "Are you sure? He's been known to roam around the woods and sometimes stake out a place to sit and think or meditate or whatever it is that he does by himself."

"No, he's missing. Cody has been taking care of him since Old Murray is recovering, and he said he never came back after their altercation and he hasn't touched his blood pressure today or yesterday."

"Oh no. Poor Topher," Aunt Astrid said.

"That's not the only problem," Jake added. "Have any of you seen Mr. Lei Park recently?"

My heart sank down to my stomach. "I saw him the day before yesterday."

Blake gave me a once-over. The look he gave me made me think he might be worried that I had been crying about something related to his case, but that quickly went away as he shifted into facts-just-the-facts mode. He pulled out his little notebook and pen.

"Where did you see him?" he asked, his voice hard and all business.

"I… was… at their house."

"What time was that?"

I rolled my eyes. "It was in the morning."

"What did you go there for? Did you have something to do with the argument he had with his wife?"

My heart that had sunk to my stomach tightened up and pounded in my ears. I knew I looked guilty of something. "Why?"

"Mrs. Park said you were there when they were having a fight. Do you know what it was about?"

I knew Blake was studying my body language, my eye movement, my tone, but I couldn't tell him the truth. I couldn't tell him about Alice Thompson. Not only would the Parks never forgive me, but I'd never forgive myself. "I did kind of arrive as something was heating up, but I was looking for Min. I only stayed for about fifteen minutes, maybe half an hour tops, then I left." It wasn't a complete lie. It was just maybe half the truth.

Blake nodded as he scribbled his notes. Then he looked at Jake as if to say he didn't think I was telling the truth, the whole truth, and nothing but the truth, so help me God.

When the two detectives left, they didn't have much more than they had started with. Jake gave Bea a wink as if to let her know he might pick her brain a little later when no one else was around. The truth was none of us knew where Topher or Mr. Park could be. Even Treacle was on edge as he nudged me and forced his head underneath my hand. He must have sensed something was wrong and wanted a little extra attention.

"Where do you think they could be?" Bea asked, looking from me to Aunt Astrid.

I shrugged, but Aunt Astrid had a very calm expression. Her chin was raised, and she looked off as if she were staring out the windows.

"They may not be there now, but they will be there later," she said. "Where everything started. In the cemetery."

"Are you sure?" Bea asked, a shiver visibly running up her spine.

"Tonight is the full moon. If the Unfamiliar is going to take another shot at raising a corpse with Mr. Park's life force as the trade, he'll try to do that tonight."

"But we're ready for it, right?" I asked.

For some reason, I felt as if I might be the weakest link in this chain, and I had never felt that way before. Some of this unrest was my fault. If I hadn't interfered with Mr. Park's personal business, he might still be home or at the shop, without any idea Topher was harboring in his head a fugitive from another dimension that was encouraging acts of violence.

When Aunt Astrid didn't reply immediately, I shook where I stood.

"So how prepared are we?" Bea asked, placing her hand gently over mine.

"We need to unite our strength," Aunt Astrid said. "This is no ordinary Unfamiliar. In fact, it is a little too familiar for my liking."

"What does that mean?" Bea's eyes bounced back and forth between Aunt Astrid and me, and it was obvious that she had been left out of something. "You can't keep a secret from me. Not now. Not when so much is going on."

"The Unfamiliar knows about my mom," I said. "It knows about the monster under my bed, and it seemed to be kind of happy about the whole situation."

Bea gasped and slapped her hand over her mouth. "Oh, Cath, what are we going to do? Maybe you shouldn't come tonight. Mom, does she have to come? Can we do this ourselves?"

"That's what I was thinking. Cath, you may have to sit this one out. Maybe you could continue a vigil to help keep the spell of protection over us. You could perform a cleansing ritual for the house to make sure nothing tries to sneak in the back door. You could—"

"Oh, no. I'm not sitting this out on the sidelines. You're both off your rockers if you think I'll do that. Even if you insisted I stay home, I'd just follow you without you noticing." I put my hands on my hips. "I've got to come.

You can't shut me out. I feel like this one is partially my fault."

I understood where they were coming from, I really did, and I couldn't shake the feeling that maybe they were right. But like the idea of letting the Parks know they were in danger, I just had it set in my head that I had to go with them. I had to help shut this door and get Topher some peace while making sure he wasn't charged for the murder of Lei Park. The idea that I might be the cause of someone else losing their life was too much to ignore. It was bad enough my own parents had died trying to protect me. It was all my fault, my fault, my fault.

Wait. Where had that thought come from? I'd never felt like that before. Something was going on inside my head, and the only way I would get to the bottom of it was to go to the cemetery tonight.

"Please," I begged. "I think... I think something is wrong with me. I can't put my finger on it, but I can feel it. Aunt Astrid, I think something is trying to break through your protection spell. I can't tell you how or why. It's just a hunch. But I'm afraid it will stay around, picking at my brain, if I don't go with you tonight. Please don't leave me behind."

"Protection spell? Why do you have a protection spell?" Bea looked at me as if I had just informed her I had a slight case of the plague.

I shrugged and smiled awkwardly.

"The Unfamiliar. It's stronger than you thought. Could it be trying to wear Cath down?" Bea asked Aunt Astrid.

The older woman nodded.

We discussed what we were going to do, and the staff relieved us in the afternoon so we could get some rest. When it was finally eight o'clock, we closed the coffee shop for the night. Aunt Astrid and Bea had decided to meet at the cemetery entrance at eleven thirty. Neither of them had given me a solid affirmative that I was to go with them, so I was left alone at my apartment with instructions to start a vigil and wait for their phone call. Darkness was coming. And it knew my face.

32. Shadows

B eing told to stay home when my "sisters" were going out to fight a battle on a spiritual level made me feel like I had gotten stood up for prom. I tried to keep the vigil. I had lit the candles in the order Aunt Astrid had instructed. I knew the words to say and at what time to say them. But my heart wasn't in it. Why couldn't I just recite them at the graveyard? Why couldn't I be there?

The minutes seemed to tick by five at a time, and before I knew it, it was already ten thirty. If I left now, I could make it to the meeting place just in time to meet Aunt Astrid and Bea. They wouldn't have any choice but to let me tag along. I decided to leave. Sure, my judgment hadn't been the best for the past two days, but unlike my experience with the Parks, I didn't feel this was the wrong thing to do. I felt it was exactly what I needed to do.

If I left right then and there, I'd make it to the cemetery just in time. Without another thought, I blew out the candles, stepped into my shoes, threw a shawl around my shoulders, and left.

The street was quiet, amazingly quiet, as if it were in a bubble. No one in Wonder Falls was outside at that hour. Usually there were some kids strolling around past curfew or couples walking hand-in-hand along the dark streets, giggling and stealing kisses when the shadows made a quick pocket of discretion. But there was no one out tonight.

A couple of homes were illuminated by the flicker of their television sets. Others had quiet music coming through open windows. It was as if they all had been told, on a subconscious level, to stay inside. So for all intents and purposes, I was alone on the street.

Or maybe I wasn't.

As I neared the cemetery entrance, the street-lights flickered. Sometimes they surged as I passed; other times they winked out completely until I had made it a couple yards away, then they'd pop back on.

The shadows appeared to be taking on life of their own. Even my own shadow, which stretched out long and lean from my feet each time I passed under a lamp, seemed to have turned on me, pulling other shadows to it and getting darker and darker. I felt that if I stared at it, I might just fall into that darkness. But I kept moving. I recited the words Aunt Astrid had told me to. I couldn't tell if they were doing any good, but I didn't want to stop chanting them for fear things might just get worse if I did. For a second, I wondered what other girls did on their Thursday nights. How many enjoyed a stroll down ever-darkening sidewalks with shadows creeping up on them? Did they welcome the occasional demon expulsion, or was it just routine to them? My internal attempts at humor weren't working.

I felt my footsteps become quicker and clap softly along the pavement with each step. Finally, I was within view of the cemetery entrance, and I saw Bea and Aunt Astrid there. They were talking, probably making a plan before they went in. As I broke into a run, I tripped and tumbled over myself, scraping my knee.

"What in the world?" I mumbled, turning around to see nothing on the ground except shadows.

At least, I thought they were shadows. But they began to writhe around my ankle like snakes. When I tried to push myself up, I felt them tighten like rubber bands, digging into my skin. Something didn't want me getting to the cemetery.

Everything inside me jumped into panic mode. All I wanted was to scream for my family and see them come running. But I couldn't yell for help without the risk of drawing attention to us. How would we explain traipsing through the cemetery at this hour? The shadows were writhing and pulling me back into a bigger pool of darkness. My knees and hands were getting terribly scratched up. I thought of my mother. This wasn't much different from the way she got dragged under my bed, except I had seen the hands, or should I say claws, that held her.

Like a bolt of lightning, the words she had been saying that day shot out of my mouth. *"Plestipacidus cum leviora."*

In an instant, the shadowy snakes recoiled, wriggling and thrashing all over themselves until they became plain, flat shadows on the pavement again.

Needless to say, I was sort of struck dumb. I hadn't thought of those words in years. The memory of my mother's voice was like an old music box wrapped up in sheets of tissue paper and stuffed into a hope chest. It was a treasure that I couldn't bear to listen to. But as I pushed myself up off the sidewalk and hurried toward my family, I felt renewed.

Everything around me appeared to become sharper and more focused, but one nagging thought remained. Why hadn't the Unfamiliar pounced on me when it had the chance at the orphanage? Aunt Astrid had already slid out of the window when it appeared at the door, yet it made no attempt to enter. It would have gotten to me before I could shimmy out the window, but it didn't even try.

And when it was speaking through Topher at the animal shelter, it had a perfect opportunity to take me out or at least give me a jolt so strong, I'd be afraid to set foot outside my home for years. Instead, it just threw out a couple of insults and low blows and scurried away. Was it weak? Had it drained its strength? Was it just waiting for the full moon?

There was an answer there. The clarity I had felt was slipping away again. Cotton was filling my head, making it hard to think. This wasn't Aunt Astrid's protection spell. Something was trying to break through it.

I gritted my teeth and ran as fast as I could to the cemetery entrance just as Bea and Aunt Astrid disappeared among the trees and tombstones.

Normally the stone structures with names and dates of loved ones from Wonder Falls never caused me any apprehension. But as I slipped between them, trying to see in what direction the other two Greenstones had gone, I felt as if I was getting lost. Things started to swim and tilt a little around me. My legs felt as if they were weighted with cement blocks, and I just wanted to sit down and rest. The headstones became large and menacing and seemed to muscle me in the opposite direction of my family. When I opened my mouth to call out to them, nothing happened.

Before I fell to the ground, I stopped and tried to steady myself. I saw a small black shadow slinking up to me. It had brilliant green eyes that looked as if they were lit from behind. I recognized those eyes.

33. The Three Witches

"Treacle," I whispered.

The black alley cat jumped into my arms and purred and rubbed his head on my chin. As I stroked his black fur, I felt my head clearing. With a deep breath, I looked into his eyes as his thick black paw tapped my chin.

"I'm so sorry. I can't hear you. Aunt Astrid's spell. It should be over soon."

He gave a quiet meow, his jowls vibrating with excitement. He pushed out of my arms with his front and back legs, and landed in the thick grass. Looking over his shoulder, he obviously wanted me to follow him.

"Where are they, Treacle? Show me," I whispered.

With that, he trotted toward the southeastern part of the cemetery.

The cemetery had about four acres of pristine land. It was a good distance away from the street, and a visitor would require a map to locate any particular grave. The tombstones that had been erected in the southeastern section, where the ground was softer and the grass was still visible in the sections of sod that were rolled out like carpet, seemed brand new and polished compared to some. My parents were between the really old section, where the stones were simple rectangles with worn, barely legible names, and these new, elegant eternal resting markers.

Thankfully, there weren't many new tombstones in these four acres. But one, flanked on both sides by two of the beautiful old oaks that grew majestically throughout the property, had been recently tended to. The dirt had barely had a chance to settle when it had been so disrespectfully disturbed.

I saw Aunt Astrid and Bea crouching behind a large tombstone with the name Smith chiseled across its face. They were watching with disgust as the man who used to be harmless Topher laughed and taunted the gravesite of Thomas Thompson while kicking and poking Lei Park's unconscious body.

I ran up to them and felt their positive energy start to chase away my vertigo. But they didn't seem all that happy to see me.

"Cath, what are you doing here?" Bea whispered angrily, grabbing my wrist and yanking me down into the shadow behind the tombstone. "You were supposed to stay home and continue the vigil."

"Yes, I know. But I couldn't—"

"Catherine, I am telling you right now to leave. Your cousin and I can handle this."

Aunt Astrid was either furious with me or the shadows made her look more angry than she actually was. I preferred to think it was the latter.

"I know you can. But I think this thing wants me to stay away. I think it might be scared of something about me. It had two perfectly good chances to get me out of the picture, yet it didn't. Why?" I held each of their hands. "You can't tell me you don't feel a little stronger now that we are all together. Right?"

Topher stopped what he was doing and glared in our direction. His lips peeled back from his teeth, and he looked nothing like the gentle hermit we knew. We were looking at a devil.

Aunt Astrid looked at Topher then back at me. Squeezing my hand, she nodded. With a fearlessness I had never seen, she marched up to Topher until she stood only about ten feet in front of him.

"You will cease your actions here, monster of the darkest dimension. Leave this place of peace and slither back down the hole you dared creep out of!" she said.

Topher's body convulsed, and his eyes rolled to the back of his head. Words came out of his gaping mouth in a voice that was not his. "Get back, old woman. Witch! While you still have a chance to live out your next few years in ignorant bliss. This host has summoned me. He has allowed me in. You slither back."

"The Maid of the Mist and the Creator of the universe condemn you back to the darkness you came from!" Bea stood and joined Aunt Astrid. Her voice was confident and strong, but her body shook as the thing inside Topher sneered and laughed at her.

Whatever it was residing inside Topher was wreaking havoc on his body. His hands were dirty and looked to be bleeding. I assumed he had used his hands to dig up poor Tommy's grave. His face was contorted into a painfully unnatural grimace, and I heard the Unfamiliar grinding and gnashing Topher's teeth, which were already in pretty bad shape after years of avoiding the dentist chair. His skin was scratched as if he had tried to get relief from hives or mosquito bites, and in some places, his skin was scratched open and bleeding a little.

It continued to laugh then spoke quickly. "You can't stop me, witch!" It leered and pointed dirty, bloody hands at them. "Don't you know what he's done? Don't you know he's invited me in?" It laughed in a freakish, almost childlike tone. "This creature summoned me. I'll do his bidding, and in return, I get his soul."

Just as I was about to join Aunt Astrid and Bea in the expulsion ceremony, with one wave of his mangled and dirty hand, the spirit in Topher brought down a huge branch from one of the thick old oaks. The branch didn't land right on them, but as she lunged out of the way, Bea's foot got pinned beneath it. She let out a cry of pain, and the Unfamiliar cried out in a mocking sort of way.

As I sat there watching, I was paralyzed with fear. What if I had been wrong? What if I should have stayed home and done what my family wanted me to? I could have totally screwed everything up by coming to the cemetery. And what did I do when the tree branch fell and Aunt Astrid lost her balance and Bea cried out in pain? I stayed right where I was. I was frozen in place. Tears filled my eyes as I thought that this was exactly how I had reacted when my mother was in trouble. I was so scared.

The Unfamiliar chanted in weird languages that I was sure were a lot older than me and Wonder Falls and maybe even the earth itself. Mr. Park wailed. His eyes were still closed, but he cried out in anguish as the words the Unfamiliar was saying began to separate Mr. Park's life force from his body.

34. Revenge

T reacle jumped onto the tombstone I was crouching behind, and he hissed at me. Never in his life had he done that. The protection spell Aunt Astrid had slapped on me must have been extra-strength, because I was still unable to communicate with any of the cats. I didn't know what Treacle was saying, but he looked at me then at the Unfamiliar. It was clear if I wasn't going to do something, *he* would. My pet cat, which had gotten into scrapes with the alley cats, was braver than me at that moment. He turned away from me and made himself known to the horrible spirit inside Topher just as I stood from my hiding place.

For a second, everything fell silent. Bea and Aunt Astrid didn't make a sound. The demon in Topher stopped and stared. The wind ceased to blow, and I swore even the crickets held their breath. My pulse was pounding in my ears. The thing was ugly, yet I stared at it.

Finally Topher let out a cry, stretching his human mouth long and wide. It wasn't the demon making that noise; it was Topher. He was still in there and in terrible pain. I could feel it. I looked at Bea, who was crying. She felt it too. She felt the suffering that the Unfamiliar was inflicting on this harmless old man more than any of us could.

Then it laughed. "So you didn't listen to your instinct and decided to come. I knew you would. Your mother said you would. She said you would." The Unfamiliar stared at me.

Aunt Astrid helped Bea pull her foot free and get to her feet.

It was trying to rattle me by talking about my mother, but I took a deep breath, held it, and walked up to the girls. I tried to look brave, but something told me I wouldn't be winning any Oscars for my performance.

Aunt Astrid and Bea took turns commanding the demon. They shouted spells and demands, but nothing was getting through. It was as if it had its own protection spell that we couldn't break through.

"It's Topher," I mumbled, my eyes widening with surprise.

The Unfamiliar began to chant its poisonous incantation. I stepped closer and looked at its dead white eyes and dirty, scratched hands and face.

"Topher! I know you're in there! I know why you did this!" I shouted over the Unfamiliar's gurgling, diabolical gibberish. "I know what you're feeling. I wanted revenge too."

The words stopped. The white eyes looked at me, and the mouth, although still moving, was no longer making noise.

The real Topher was listening, and I was sure the Unfamiliar was afraid of me. It hadn't wanted me there because I had the power to get through to Topher.

"I did, Topher. I wanted revenge. Why did my mother and father have to die? What did I do that was so bad I should be left alone? I didn't even get to say good-bye." My eyes filled with tears. I couldn't help it. "I didn't get to say 'I love you' one more time. Yes, I wanted revenge."

"Revenge," Topher hissed.

"And I thought about all the people who were mean to me. The people who were cruel and nasty, yet still they had both of their parents. Maybe I should be cruel and nasty too, right? Maybe that was what the world needed. Maybe if I just called for some help, I'd get it. It didn't matter who from. Then I could have revenge. And once I got revenge, Topher, what would I have left?"

Topher shook his head like a dog after it gets out of a sudsy bath. His expression was confused and almost embarrassed.

"I wouldn't have anything left. I wouldn't have my parents any more than you'd get Tommy back. I wouldn't get even with those mean girls any more than you'll even the score with Mr. Park. You don't want to do this, Topher. Death is a part of life. It's the part that makes us cherish our memories."

"No. No. No," the Unfamiliar hissed.

"It's the part that makes us value each day. To try to reverse the natural course of life is to hand ourselves over to the evil one. You're just sad, Topher. It's okay. It's okay to be sad and angry. But if you don't fight it, you'll feel a part of you die slowly every day as hatred consumes you. Please." I clenched my fists and stood up straight. "Fight it!"

"No. No. No," it hissed. "No. No. No." Its voice was quick, and it took three fast steps toward me.

I flinched a little but recovered and stood my ground. I looked into its eyes as a thin string of drool dripped out of the corner of its slackened jaw. For a flash, Topher's gentle old eyes appeared.

"I see you, Topher. Don't let it win. Tell it to go. Tell it to leave!"

Just as quickly, his eyes became strange again. It threw its head back and cried a pitiful, painful howl.

"Leave me." The words sounded as if they were being choked out.

My heart broke for the old man. The hatred I felt for this evil spirit was palpable. It fed off the emotions of humans who were beyond sad, beyond hopeless. I wanted to take Topher's hands and hold them, but I didn't dare.

"Leave me alone!" Again Topher spoke, his voice slightly stronger.

I could only imagine the pain he was going through. Removing the Unfamiliar was like pulling one of those spiny, prickly weeds out by the roots. Their tentacles wove through the dirt, spreading out until they consumed everything around them. Nothing but sheer will would get them loose. Right now, that was what Topher was doing. He was pulling this weed from his soul, and it was hurting him for it.

"Leave me alone! Leave me alone! Now! Now!"

Suddenly he stopped. For a minute, I thought he was dead on his feet. I stared at his eyes, which had snapped shut. I looked for his chest to rise and fall with breath. Any twitch of his hands or face. But there was nothing. He just stood stone still.

"I'm afraid!" Topher cried to me. "I'm afraid." He whimpered as tears dragged dirt down his cheeks.

"You should be," I spat back, recognizing the trick of the Unfamiliar.

Taking one step back, I reached out my hands. Bea took one, and Aunt Astrid took the other. Like pulling a bent, twisted, rusty nail from a board, we recited the expulsion chant. The Unfamiliar contorted poor Topher as it tried to stay inside him. It scratched at his body and made him fall to the ground, writhing like a maggot in hot sun. But we didn't stop. We chanted until our throats were scratchy and our palms sweaty from holding on to each other.

Finally, the Unfamiliar couldn't take any more. Topher tossed his head back violently, and the Unfamiliar flew from his mouth until it became a long black serpent hovering over him in the air. Its eyes were a sickly orange color with black pupils, and it rolled its tongue around its face like a lizard licks its own eyeballs. It screamed.

"Gamodan! Ex! Enfinitu!" Aunt Astrid cried. "You will cease your actions here, monster of the darkest dimension! Leave this place of peace and slither back down the hole you dared creep out of!"

In its true state, the Unfamiliar crinkled up as if it were being burned. Folding around and over itself, it became smaller and smaller until it was the size of a golf ball. With a loud clap like a door slamming and the sound of glass shattering, it was over.

Topher fell to the ground, crying. Bea rushed to his side, and he looked at her with red eyes and wet with tears.

"I didn't get a chance to tell him how proud I was of him," he mumbled. "I just wanted one minute, just one more minute to tell him that."

Bea put her arms around the old man.

To him, it was just a hug, an opportunity to literally cry on someone's shoulder. To her, it was a chance to see some of his ailments caused by his grief. The Unfamiliar had filled his mind with so many whispers that it was probably clouded over like an extra membrane had developed around it. His heart was already grief stricken, but the guilt the Unfamiliar had poured onto him pierced his heart like thousands of tiny thorns. While Bea spoke gently, soothing his worries, she worked diligently to pull away the fibrous remains of the Unfamiliar's brain haze and pull the barbs from his heart one at a time. With each passing minute, he became more peaceful until he fell asleep with Bea's arm around him.

"What about Mr. Park?" Bea asked, jerking her head in his direction.

"He's still out cold. I think they're both sleeping," Aunt Astrid said.

Bea nodded in relief. Non-witches recuperated from encounters with the supernatural by shutting down. In the morning, what they'd seen, heard, felt could be easily waved away as part of some lucid dream. Us Greenstones, on the other hand, would feel as if we had drunk moonshine straight from a homemade pressure cooker still, and that would stick with us for a couple of days.

35. Image Ruined

I called Jake to tell him that we had found Mr. Park and Topher. He and Blake arrived with an ambulance ready to take both men to the hospital.

Blake marched right up to me even though Aunt Astrid and Bea were both standing just a couple feel from me. "How did you know they were here?"

"I, uh, didn't know they were here, Detective. As you know, my parents are buried in this cemetery, and I wanted to visit."

"In the middle of the night?"

"I couldn't sleep."

"We decided to come together," Aunt Astrid interrupted. "I also wanted to say hi to my late husband when Cath couldn't sleep, so we decided to make it a family outing."

"With Bea?"

"She's very supportive," Aunt Astrid said. "We heard Mr. Park trying to get Topher to leave his grandson's grave and go home. Mr. Park was telling him how worried Cody was, but Topher was just inconsolable. By the time we could see what was going on, Mr. Park tried to lead Topher away, but the old man jerked his hand away. When he did, Mr. Park lost his balance, and down he went. Hit his head. Topher just crumpled… from grief, I'd guess. You ever lose someone close to you, Detective?"

So it wasn't the greatest story ever told. As I watched Blake's eyes, I was positive if he didn't slap cuffs on all three of us, he would string us up in straitjackets. But he didn't do either.

After he finished writing everything, he went over to Bea, who was sitting on the SMITH tombstone that just a short while ago we were all hiding behind. She was cradling her foot, and her toes had swollen to two times their original size. Jake knelt in front of her, talking to her quietly as Blake approached.

"Is that what happened?" Blake asked firmly.

Nothing makes you feel like a liar more than having someone check your story right in front of you.

"Yes, Blake. It is," Bea said gently.

Without another word, he nodded, folded up his notebook, stuffed it into his shirt pocket, and looked at me. I wasn't sure why his eyes roamed up and down my body, but I felt a blush rush over me. Placing one hand on my hip, I gave him my best *what now* look.

He didn't say a word but turned back to Jake and Bea. "Better get that looked at." He pointed at poor Bea's gigantic foot. "How did it happen?"

"I was running to help and tripped over poor Mrs. Marconi over there." Bea pointed at one of the flat rectangular tombstones. One edge peeked up over the grass just high enough to cause a person not looking to trip.

And what did Blake do after she said that? Did he turn to Aunt Astrid or me and ask if that were true? Did he study her up and down as if she were some kind of lying machine? Nope. He just nodded and gave me another once-over.

"We're going to the hospital," Jake said, sweeping all one hundred twenty pounds of Bea into his arms. Slowly he made his way between the graves, and I heard Bea giggling just a little as he spoke to her.

"Can I give you ladies a lift home?" Blake asked, looking more at Aunt Astrid than me.

"Absolutely not—"

"That would be nice of you, Detective," Aunt Astrid said. "It has been a long night, and I just don't feel like walking anymore."

She slipped her arm through his, and I saw him ruffle just a little at being touched. He didn't dare say anything to Aunt Astrid though, who began asking him a dozen questions about his job.

I thought about Topher and hoped that Mr. Park would have enough of a magic hangover that our story would sound like what really happened. An argument. A tussle. No attempts at raising another corpse. No minion of Hades taking over an old man's body. The whole thing was nothing but a simple misunderstanding and bad footing.

Blake let Aunt Astrid sit in the front of the car where his partner usually sat. I sat in the back where the doors locked and couldn't be opened from the inside. I felt like a teenager embarrassed of everything and anything. Within a few minutes, we were in front of Aunt Astrid's place. Blake opened the back door, and I climbed out as Aunt Astrid made her way up her front porch steps.

"I'd be happy to take you to your apartment. It's on the way to the station," he said in that annoying just-the-facts manner. Even when he said he was happy, it always ended up sounding sarcastic. I never knew what he was really feeling.

"Uh, no. I'm going to sleep here. Truth is, I probably won't be able to sleep much after all that."

Blake nodded again as he looked at the pavement. "So you go to the cemetery at night on full moons. Why?"

I couldn't believe it. He was still digging. I had to make my lie a good one.

"I told you—I couldn't sleep. But the truth is, I don't like people to see me get emotional. No one except family. Even though my parents have been gone for a good while, it still hurts. I just don't want anyone to see me like that. So I go at night, and Aunt Astrid and Bea come with so no one will bother me. Strength in numbers, you know."

"Yes, I do." He looked at me. His eyes were intense, and in the dark, with just the full moon shining on one side of his face and Aunt Astrid's warm yellow porch light lighting up the other side, I thought for a second he looked downright handsome. "Well, I'll be in touch. There might be a few more questions."

I rolled my eyes. "Don't worry," I said as I stepped around him to follow my aunt into her home. "I won't plan on taking any long trips across the border any time soon."

What was I thinking? Handsome… maybe. But then he opened his mouth and spoke. Whole image ruined.

36. Don't Mess With Texas

The next morning, Bea hobbled into the Brew-Ha-Ha on crutches with a cast on her foot, signed with a big heart with arrows going through it and Jake's name written in big letters inside it.

"I can't believe it," I said as she hopped behind the counter next to me. "You make a plaster cast look fashionable. How do you do it?"

Bea let out a sarcastic chuckle and bumped me with her hip.

My eyes searched her face. "Did you tell Jake what really happened?"

"I did."

"And?"

"And he said he'd convince Blake to leave Samantha Perry's death unsolved," she said.

"I think that might be kind of hard. Blake was grilling me last night after he dropped us off at Aunt Astrid's house. He's like a dog with a bone."

"Oh, he dropped you off, did he?" Bea pulled a stack of napkins from behind the counter and stuffed them in one of the silver boxes along the counter.

I scrunched my eyebrows together. "What?"

"He kept checking in the rearview mirror as if he thought she might fall out of the car," Aunt Astrid added as she placed a pecan pie on the pretty wire display on the counter.

"I don't know what you two are talking about."

They both giggled like schoolgirls, and I couldn't tell what for. If Blake had been looking at me, it was because he didn't believe what any of us had told him and was plotting how to catch us.

"Aren't either one of you worried that he's going to keep snooping around until he finds something? Something about *us*?" I said.

"Well, if he does, he won't have anything from last night to help his case. I conjured a mirroring spell over that part of the cemetery. The other dimensions that cross over that area will bounce off each other, making it all look smooth and undisturbed. He won't be able to find so much as a footprint. Not even his own."

I took a deep breath. I was happy to hear that. Treacle jumped on my lap and purred.

"It's all right," I told him. *"I can hear you now."*

Being unable to talk to me had been strange for him, and he became a little more affectionate now. I think a part of him didn't take our communication for granted anymore.

Treacle's wounds were fading. It turned out he'd gotten into a fight at the old orphanage. He'd been snooping around and ran into that nasty street cat who seemed to be the gatekeeper. Treacle found out from the street cat that the Unfamiliar was bigger and badder, but he couldn't tell me when I had the protection spell on. I rubbed his ears.

Min's smiley face peeked in underneath the open sign that hung on the front door. He knocked gently on the glass. Smiling, I waved him in.

"Oh, and number two makes an appearance," Bea teased, making Aunt Astrid laugh.

"You two can shut up now," I grumbled as Min opened the door and strolled up to the counter.

"Hello, ladies," he said with a smile.

"Good morning. You sure are in a good mood," I said, bumping Bea intentionally with my hip. "Considering…" Considering that his missing father had gone to the hospital last night.

"I'm just glad we found my dad," Min said, understanding what I meant. "And that he's safe. He's going to be fine."

"That's great," Bea said.

"That's not all," Min said. "I have amazing news."

"Oh, then wait." I grabbed one of the many eclectic coffee mugs we had lined up underneath the counter. The one I grabbed said "Mother, put the tea on." I'd never quite understood it, but it seemed to fit in in our odd little shop. I filled it with hot water and picked out an Earl Gray tea bag that I dropped in the steaming water.

Min wrapped his hands around the cup and took the seat across from me. "I'm reforming the Wonder Falls nursing home. I just got through talking with the director. We drew up the paperwork right then and there. I'm now on the board of directors, which consists of the librarian, a guy from the post office, and David Wayne of the law firm Wayne, Van Driska, and Associates."

"Is that good?"

"It's great! And not only am I on the board of directors, but my father has offered to provide some goods from his store every month at no charge."

My face screwed up in a confused grimace, but Min shook his head as if he was in as much shock as I was.

"I know what you're thinking," he said. "But after I went with my mother to see him in the hospital last night, it was like we met a different man. All he would say was that he and Topher had a talk. That was it. Him and that hermit."

I looked at Bea and Aunt Astrid, who shrugged and went back to wiping off the small tables at the front of the coffee shop.

"Did he say what they talked about?" I asked carefully.

"No. But I did hear him speaking in Korean to my mother. He usually only does that when he's mad, but I could tell by his tone he wasn't mad. It was hard to hear him since I wasn't in the same room, but I caught the gist of it. He was saying something about being sorry and how things would be different. But after my mother left, her cheeks glowed."

I couldn't help but feel happy for Min. It was nice that whatever Mr. Park remembered about last night wouldn't be an issue for us. I could only guess that he and Topher had resolved to put the past behind them. It must've been painful, carrying that secret for all those years. I wondered how Mr. Park could bear to see Thomas in this town, but maybe Topher didn't allow them to see each other. Mr. Park would have had to respect Topher's wishes.

"And, as if that isn't great enough," Min said.

"There's more?"

"Yes."

"Well, in that case." I grabbed a cup for myself. It had the flag of Texas on one side and the words "Don't mess with Texas" written in a rope on the other. After pouring in some hot water, I dropped in a tea bag for myself.

"Topher," Min said.

I felt my heart jump in my throat. "What about him?"

"Well, he and Cody and I talked in the hospital too. My father has agreed to sponsor him. As soon as he's released, he'll move into his new apartment at the Wonder Falls Retirement Community."

"Oh, Min, what a nice gesture."

"You know, it's the least I could do for the man who talked my father into changing."

I smiled broadly. "This really is amazing."

I was glad the past few months were behind us. The Unfamiliar was gone for now, and it was still a mystery. Did it know the Unfamiliar under my bed? Would it ever come back? We would have to see. But for now, I wanted to enjoy a moment of peace in my hometown.

"I know. I tell you, Cath, I can't believe how things have turned out. You just never know how life is going to twist and turn and…"

Min talked with me through the morning rush, and I was happy to listen. It was almost as if the Unfamiliar had been just a tiny detail mixed in with all of the miracles that seemed to pop up like new buds after a long winter.

About the Author

Harper Lin is the bestselling the author of *The Patisserie Mysteries*, *The Emma Wild Holiday Mysteries*, *The Wonder Cats Mysteries*, and *The Cape Bay Cafe Mysteries*.

When she's not reading or writing mysteries, she loves going to yoga classes, hiking, and hanging out with her family and friends.

www.HarperLin.com

Pawsitively Dead

CPSIA information can be obtained at www.ICGtesting.com
Printed in the USA
LVOW10s1548231015

459498LV00005B/506/P